DOGS TELL THEIR OWN STORIES

DOGS TELL THEIR OWN STORIES

EDITED BY ELIZABETH RATISSEAU

DARLING & COMPANY

MCMXCIX

DARLING & COMPANY
POST OFFICE BOX 4399
SEATTLE   WASHINGTON   98104
800.354.0400

TABLE OF CONTENTS

TABLE OF CONTENTS

PREFACE

Many dogs have written (or dictated) autobiographical narratives, and this volume contains a selection of them. No other animal has a similar confessional impulse. Even cats, who outnumber dogs as pets, seldom write. I do know of one rat's autobiography, and several by horses.

What I have discovered, in studying dog literature, is that dogs are nearly as various as humans in their likes and dislikes, literary skill, empathetic power, and reaction to circumstances.

Dogs have a particular passion for poetry, and though they seldom venture beyond simple forms, they do frequently achieve eloquence and concision.

In reading the many books by dogs from which this book was sifted, I have been delighted, touched, and most of all, broadened by the fresh perspectives offered by our usually mute companions.

MEMOIRS OF A YELLOW DOG

AS TOLD TO O. HENRY

I don't suppose it will knock any of you people off your perch to read a contribution from an animal. Mr. Kipling and a good many others have demonstrated the fact that animals can express themselves in remunerative English, and no magazine goes to press nowadays without an animal story in it, except the old-style monthlies that are still running pictures of Bryan and the Mont Pelée horror.

But you needn't look for any stuck-up literature in my piece, such as Bearoo, the bear, and Snakoo, the snake, and Tammanoo, the tiger, talk in the jungle books. A yellow dog that's spent most of his life in a cheap New York flat, sleeping in a corner on an old sateen underskirt (the one she spilled wine on at the Lady Longshoremen's banquet), mustn't be expected to perform any tricks with the art of speech.

I was born a yellow pup; date, locality, pedigree, and weight unknown. The first thing I can recollect, an old woman had me in a basket at Broadway and Twenty-third trying to sell me to a fat lady. Old Mother Hubbard was boosting me to bear the band as a genuine Pomeranian-Hambletonian Red-Irish-Cochin-China-Stoke-Pogis fox terrier. The fat lady chased a V around among the samples of grosgrain flannelette in her shopping bag till she cornered it, and gave up. From that moment on I was a pet—a mamma's own wootsey squidlums. Say, gentle reader, did you ever have a two-hundred pound woman breathing a flavor of Camembert cheese and Peau d'Espagne pick you up and wallop her nose all over you, remarking all the time in an Emma Eames

tone of voice: "Oh, oo's um oodlum, doodlum, woodlum, tood-
lum, bitsy-witsy skoodlums?"

From a pedigreed yellow pup I grew up to be an anonymous
yellow cur looking like a cross between an Angora cat and a box
of lemons. But my mistress never tumbled. She thought that the
two primeval pups that Noah chased into the ark were but a col-
lateral branch of my ancestors. It took two policeman to keep her
from entering me at the Madison Square Garden for the Siberian
bloodhound prize.

I'll tell you about that flat. The house was the ordinary thing
in New York, paved with Parian marble in the entrance hall and
cobblestones above the first floor. Our flat was three f—well, not
flights—climbs up. My mistress rented it unfurnished, and put in
the regular things—1903 antique upholstered parlor set, oil chro-
mo of geishas in a Harlem teahouse, rubber plant, and husband.

By Sirius! There was a biped I felt sorry for. He was a little
man with sandy hair and whiskers a good deal like mine.
Henpecked? Well, toucans and flamingos and pelicans all had
their bills in him. He wiped the dishes and listened to my mistress tell about the cheap, ragged things the lady with the squir-
rel-skin coat on the second floor hung out on her line to dry. And
every evening while she was getting supper she made him take me
out on the end of a string for a walk.

If men knew how women pass the time when they are alone
they'd never marry. Laura Jean Libbey, peanut brittle, a little
almond cream on the neck muscles, dishes unwashed, half an
hour's talk with the iceman, reading a package of old letters, a
couple of pickles and two bottles of malt extract, one hour peek-
ing through a hole in the window shade into the flat across the air
shaft—that's about all there is to it. Twenty minutes before time
for him to come home from work she straightens up the house,

fixes her rat so it won't show, and gets out a lot of sewing for a ten-minute bluff.

I led a dog's life in that flat. 'Most all day I lay there in my corner watching that fat woman kill time. I slept sometimes and had pipe dreams about being out chasing cats into basements and growling at old ladies with black mittens, as a dog was intended to do. Then she would pounce upon me with a lot of that driveling poodle palaver and kiss me on the nose—but what could I do? A dog can't chew cloves.

I began to feel sorry for Hubby, dog my cats if I didn't. We looked so much alike that people noticed it when we went out; so we shook the streets that Morgan's cab drives down, and took to climbing the piles of last December's snow on the streets where cheap people live.

One evening when we were thus promenading, and I was trying to look like a prize Saint Bernard, and the old man was trying to look like he wouldn't have murdered the first organgrinder he heard play Mendelssohn's wedding march, I looked up at him and said, in my way:

"What are you looking so sour about, you oakum-trimmed lobster? She don't kiss you. You don't have to sit on her lap and listen to talk that would make the book of a musical comedy sound like the maxims of Epictetus. You ought to be thankful you're not a dog. Brace up, Benedick, and bid the blues begone."

The matrimonial mishap looked down at me with almost canine intelligence on his face.

"Why, doggie," says he, "good doggie. You almost look like you could speak. What is it, doggie—cats?"

Cats! Could speak!

But, of course, he couldn't understand. Humans were denied the speech of animals. The only common ground of communication upon which dogs and men can get together is in fiction.

In the flat across the hall from us lived a lady with a black-and-tan terrier. Her husband strung it and took it out every evening, but he always came home cheerful and whistling. One day I touched noses with the black-and-tan in the hall, and I struck him for an elucidation.

"See here, Wiggle-and-Skip," I says, "you know that it ain't the nature of a real man to play dry nurse to a dog in public. I never saw one leashed to a bowwow yet that didn't look like he'd like to lick every other man that looked at him. But your boss comes in every day as perky and set up as an amateur prestidigitator doing the egg trick. How does he do it? Don't tell me he likes it."

"Him?" says the black-and-tan. "Why, he uses Nature's Own Remedy. He gets spifflicated. At first when we go out he's as shy as the man on the steamer who would rather play pedro when they make 'em all jackpots. By the time we've been in eight saloons he don't care whether the thing on the end of his line is a dog or a catfish. I've lost two inches of my tail trying to sidestep those swinging doors."

The pointer I got from that terrier—vaudeville, please copy—set me to thinking.

One evening about six o'clock my mistress ordered him to get busy and do the ozone act for Lovey. I have concealed it until now, but that is what she called me. The black-and-tan was called "Tweetness." I consider that I have the bulge on him as far as you could chase a rabbit. Still, "Lovey" is something of a nomenclatural tin can on the tail of one's self-respect.

At a quiet place on a safe street I tightened the line of my custodian in front of an attractive, refined saloon. I made a dead-ahead scramble for the doors, whining like a dog in the press dispatches that lets the family know that little Alice is bogged while gathering lilies in the brook.

"Why, darn my eyes," says the old man, with a grin, "darn my eyes if the saffron-colored Son of a seltzer lemonade ain't asking me in to take a drink. Lemme see—how long's it been since I saved shoe leather by keeping one foot on the footrest? I believe I'll..."

I knew I had him. Hot Scotches he took, sitting at a table. For an hour he kept the Campbells coming. I sat by his side rapping for the waiter with my tail, and eating free lunch such as mamma in her flat never equaled with her homemade truck bought at a delicatessen store eight minutes before papa comes home.

When the products of Scotland were all exhausted except the rye bread the old man unwound me from the table leg and played me outside like a fisherman plays a salmon. Out there he took off my collar and threw it into the street. "Poor doggie," says he, "good doggie. She shan't kiss you any more. 'Sa darned shame. Good doggie, go away and get run over by a streetcar and be happy."

I refused to leave. I leaped and frisked around the old man's legs happy as a pug on a rug.

"You old flea-headed woodchuck-chaser," I said to him, "you moon-baying, rabbit-pointing, egg-stealing old beagle, can't you see that I don't want to leave you? Can't you see that we're both Pups in the Wood and the missus is the cruel uncle after you with the dish towel and me with the flea liniment and a pink bow to tie on my tail. Why not cut that all out and be pards forever more?"

Maybe you'll say he didn't understand—maybe he didn't. But he kind of got a grip on the Hot Scotches, and stood still for a minute, thinking.

"Doggie," says he, finally, "we don't live more than a dozen lives on this earth, and very few of us live to be more than three hundred. If I ever see that flat any more I'm a flat, and if you do you're flatter; and that's no flattery. I'm offering sixty to one that Westward Ho wins out by the length of a dachshund."

There was no string, but I frolicked along with my master to the Twenty-third Street ferry. And the cats on the route saw reason to give thanks that prehensile claws had been given them.

On the Jersey side my master said to a stranger who stood eating a currant bun:

"Me and my doggie, we are bound for the Rocky Mountains."

But what pleased me most was when my old man pulled both of my ears until I howled, and said:

"You common, monkey-headed, rat-tailed, sulphur-colored son of doormat, do you know what I'm go going to call you?"

I thought of "Lovey," and I whined dolefully.

I'm going to call you 'Pete,' says my master; and if I'd had five tails I couldn't have done enough wagging to do justice to the occasion.

FROM A DOG'S LIFE

BY BOY

AS TOLD TO PETER MAYLE

ADVICE TO THE YOUNG DOG

1. Beware of Christmas. It is traditionally a time when puppies are brought into the happy home as gifts. If they manage to survive an early diet of turkey, mince pies, liqueur chocolates, wrapping paper, tinsel, and tree ornaments, they grow, as puppies do. For some reason this causes astonishment and consternation among the older members of the family, who should have known better. But they don't, and by spring they're looking for someone prepared to take over a dog that has become an inconvenience. Christmas puppies should not make long-term plans. Sad but true.

2. Do not even attempt to understand the lure of television. I like to think of myself as fairly sophisticated, able to move freely among different social groups, sympathetic to their interests, however bizarre, and so forth. But here I am baffled. A box filled with small and noisy people, a disagreeable scent of heated plastic, the room plunged into darkness, conversation banned, and the faint sounds of snoring in the background—is this enjoyable? I can't make head or tail of it myself. Have you ever seen rabbits hypnotized by flashlight? That's television, as far as I'm concerned. For drama and entertainment, give me ants any day.

3. You may one night be disturbed by the stealthy arrival through the window of gentlemen who tiptoe around the house in silence. These are burglars. Never bark at them. They have no respect for animal rights and can be violent. Postpone making

any noise until they are safely out of the house. With luck, they might have taken the television.

4. The etiquette of bathing confused me for several months, but the rules seem to be as follows. It is acceptable for people to immerse themselves in water every day; indeed, they consider it a virtue and a joy. They sing; they play games with the soap; they emerge pink and glowing and pleased with themselves. Seeing this, the novice dog who wishes to please may be tempted to follow their example by taking a refreshing squirm in a puddle. This is not acceptable. Neither is shaking oneself dry in the living room or cleaning the facial hair with a brisk rub on the carpet. As in most aspects of life, a dual standard operates here, and it doesn't favor those of us with four legs and a muddy gusset.

5. Learn to distinguish between natural friends and natural enemies. I always warm to gardeners (because we have a mutual interest in digging), clumsy eaters, those who understand the principles of bribery to ensure good behavior, and denture wearers, who find biscuits difficult. To be treated with caution: anyone dressed in white, people who make patronizing inquiries about your pedigree, grumpy old men with sticks, and vegetarians (except at mealtimes when there is meat on the table that they wish to dispose of discreetly). To be avoided: women who carry photographs of their cats. They are beyond hope.

6. Recognize the need for selective obedience. Under normal circumstances, you can do more or less what you like. Man's innate idleness and short attention span will save you from too much discipline. But there will be moments of crisis when it pays to respond to a call from the authorities. You can always tell. Voices are raised, hysteria looms, and threats are uttered. When they shout in capital letters—as in "BOY! DAMNIT!"—return to base immediately, pretending you didn't hear the first time. Wag

sincerely, and all will be well.

7. Do not bring friends of the opposite sex home. This will only encourage indelicate speculation about your intentions, and it may lead to a period of house arrest. Romance, in my view, is best conducted on neutral ground, where you're unlikely to find yourself cornered and you can retain what is known these days as "maximum deniability." Follow the example of our eminent leaders: Admit to nothing until your accusers have you by the short hairs.

8. Never bite vets, even when attacked from behind by a chilly thermometer. They mean well.

9. Finally, remember that we live in an imperfect world. People make mistakes. Cocktail parties, pale-colored furniture, hair transplants, New Year's Eve, worming tablets, vibrant orange Lycra, diamanté dog collars, jogging, grooming, telephone sex, leg waxing—the list is long, and life is short. My advice is to make the best of it, and to make allowances. To err is human. To forgive, canine.

confessions of a glutton
BY PETE THE PUP
AS TOLD TO DON MARQUIS

after i ate my dinner then i ate
part of a shoe
i found some archies by a bathroom pipe
and ate them too
i ate some glue
i ate a bone that had got nice and ripe
six weeks buried in the ground
i ate a little mousie that i found
i ate some sawdust from the cellar floor
it tasted sweet
i ate some outcast meat
and some roach paste by the pantry door
and then the missis had some folks to tea
nice folks who petted me
and so i ate
cakes from a plate
i ate some polish that they use
for boots and shoes
and then i went back to the missis swell tea party
i guess i must have eat too hearty

of something maybe cake
for then came the earthquake
you should have seen the missis face
and when the boss came in she said
no wonder that dog hangs his head
he knows hes in disgrace
i am a well intentioned little pup
but sometimes things come up
to get a little dog in bad
and now i feel so very very sad
but the boss said never mind old scout
time wears disgrace out

HOUSE DOG
AS TOLD TO GEORGE BOAS

I have achieved the life of contemplation,
My paws are clean, I have not touched the mire,
I do not bark and yelp in irritation
But wait for satisfaction I require.
Life may pass by, the months pile higher and higher,
I am secure: two meals a day, a carriage
In which to take the air, a pleasant fire
To dream before, and periodic marriage.
I have anaesthetized all my ambition
And paradoxically some other's;
Existence has become a noble mission—
Admiring me, competitors and brothers,
And when they pin a ribbon on my neck
Feel it to be themselves they thus bedeck.

FROM THE INTELLIGENT DOG'S GUIDE
TO PEOPLE-OWNING
BY GREYFRIARS FLANNEL PETTICOAT
AS TOLD TO ROLAND BROWNE

PEOPLE AND THEIR LIMITATIONS

Unfortunately, there are many oversentimental People-Lovers among us who are all too eager to ascribe canine traits and reactions to their beloved charges and even insist that there are no essential differences between Dogs and People. Nothing, however, could be further from the truth. Even the most ardent People-Lover must admit, if he will face reality, that People are different from Dogs; they do not begin to understand things that even the dullest member of our race finds obvious and self-evident.

I hate to admit it, but they can't even understand things that are plain to *cats!*

Now, having said the worst about these lovable creatures, how can I explain their deficiencies of understanding? For they are wonderfully clever in some ways, and yet exasperatingly dull in others.

Try to imagine, if you will, what it would be like to have no sense of smell, or so little as to be practically smell-blind. Two People, meeting in the dark, cannot identify each other. Unbelievable? Yet it is painfully true. A Person coming into a room would not know that another Person had previously been in it, or, more important, that another was hiding in it. They can only follow visible footprints, such as might be left in snow or mud.

Most of their intelligence seems to reside in their front paws, with which they constantly manipulate and verify the obvious facts of their environment. They rely heavily on their eyes, which appear to be more acute than ours, but they invariably prefer to test what they see, or think they see, by feeling with their front paws. Observe, also, that when two of them meet, under situations where we would touch noses, they join their front paws briefly.

So heavy is their dependence upon the sense of touch that when one of them cannot grasp an idea (*grasp*, you see how one can fall into their mode of expression!) he will say that it is *intangible*. We would say that it was *odorless*.

They identify the sex of other Persons almost wholly by visual means, but this method is rather uncertain, since the females often dress exactly like the males. Apparently to make sure that their sex is recognizable, the females apply various evil-smelling substances to their bodies which the males, with their feeble sense of smell, find attractive. Fortunately, few of the males make use of these disgusting substances; and in many respects being much more like us than the females, they often have a pronounced body odor that is heady and satisfying. Young males are particularly pleasant and stimulating to smell.

Because their sense of smell is so pitifully undeveloped, they are quite unable to appreciate many of the most exquisite odors that an all-generous Creator has provided for our pleasure. Even my own special Person, who is exceptionally well-attuned to the feelings and sensibilities of Dogs, and who understands much of what I tell him, shows a definite prejudice against my enjoyment of some of the really rare odors that one all too seldom encounters. For example, there was the matter last summer of the well-ripened chicken...

The silly thing had been squawking and pecking and scratching in a thicket behind the barn, eating some kind of seeds, when I first noticed it, and when I came up behind it and greeted it courteously in the traditional canine manner, it ran shrieking and leaping on its hind paws and flapped its front paws in the most amusing and stimulating way, and when I tried to make it stay still, its tail fur, which is much broader and stiffer than ours, came out. At last I leaped upon it and threw it up in the air a number of times to discourage it from running about, so that I could examine it more readily, and then it would not run any more, and the death smell came on it. I scratched dirt over it and marked it carefully as mine, and marked several spots nearby, and went away from there, and I never mentioned the matter to my Person, but I went back to check on it every morning, and after a long time it was ready, having changed from an absurd useless bird into a lovely brown jelly with a most celestial and soul-satisfying odor. I rolled in it for a long time, paying particular attention to getting the jelly well down into the undercoat at the back of my neck, which is very difficult to do properly, and on the area immediately above the base of my tail, which is comparatively easy to accomplish.

My Person was most unreasonable when I ran joyfully to him to let him smell me; he spoke harshly to me and would not lay his paws on me after the first touch, and if I had not guessed his intent and swum for a long time in the horsepond, he would have bathed me, which is the ultimate indignity, endurable only because of the exquisite combing and scratching and brushing that always follow the bath.

Imagine, if you can, the handicap under which these poor, smell-blind creatures labor from birth to death, deprived of the most informative, the most subtle, the most glorious of our senses, and you will understand many of their innate weaknesses. And, understanding, you will be more ready to forgive their faults.

It is a moot question whether the human animal has always been without a workable sense of smell. There are those who argue that among primitive humans this sense is not wholly undeveloped, but that it is enfeebled through disuse among the more highly bred specimens that most of us keep. Certainly the absurd human habit of walking erect upon the hind legs places the nose so far above the ground as to render its serious use impracticable, and herein may lie a clue to why most adult humans have such a poorly developed olfactory sense. Very young humans do not walk erect but adopt a more sensible quadrupedal form of locomotion with the head in reasonable proximity to the ground, and it is my observation that the young appear to have a keener sense of smell than the adults, sniffing and tasting everything that their front paws encounter, and seeming to enjoy many of the headier odors and flavors that we Dogs find delightful. Unfortunately the adults do everything possible to discourage their young from this healthy exploration of their environment, so that by the time they are ready to imitate the erect gait of their parents, they have developed absurd feelings of guilt about the enjoyment of the sense of smell, desist from further experimentation, and ultimately lose what little olfactory acuity they had developed.

Not only are People unable to use their noses for any practical purposes, but their ears are of little use to them. Any thoughtful Dog will immediately recognize the absurdity of the structure of their external ears, which are ridiculously small, as though cropped like a Boxer's, and which can neither be erected to catch distant sounds, folded to keep out the rain, nor laid back to express affection. In most People, in fact, the external ear is quite paralyzed, so that when one of them can make even the most rudimentary movement of his ears he is regarded as a wag of singular accomplishment.

Perhaps because their external ears are almost vestigial, their sense of hearing is dull and weak. Another Person can trudge up to the front door and knock thunderously before a Person inside will be aware of his arrival, whereas any Dog would have heard his approach from half a mile away.

Not only are sounds of normal intensity inaudible to People, but some very high-pitched sounds simply do not exist for them. The familiar high whine, even higher than the cry of the bat, that is produced by tires of rapidly moving cars is as silence to them, and they cannot understand why we are impelled to chase after cars to catch and punish the *sound*. When the car stops, the sound stops, and so we lose interest, since it is the sound we pursue, not the car. No Person can properly understand this even if it is carefully explained to him; not even my special Person, who is quite unreasonable on this matter.

Though their eyesight is better than ours by day, they are almost blind at night, floundering around in dark rooms, falling over chairs and sleeping Dogs, bumping into doors, and generally behaving in a manner that would appear imbecilic to the average Dog, accustomed to seeing almost as well by night as by day, and aided immensely by his sense of smell. It is to be hoped that Dogs who are new to Person-Owning will take this night blindness of People into account and make allowances for what is, after all, a deficiency that People are born with, and for which they should not be blamed.

Dingo, the German Shepherd bitch with whom I share my Person, seems quite unable to grasp this deficiency of his, and when he steps on her tail in the dark—it is a ridiculously long, flapping appendage anyhow, always in the way, unlike my own neatly bobbed tail—she shrieks and complains most unreasonably, taking the mishap as a deliberate affront or an unprovoked attack.

I have spoken about the deficiencies of the human animal in the matter of his senses of smell and hearing. If what I have said is surprising to those of you who are new to Person-Owning, you may find it all but incredible that People, with very few exceptions, are devoid of the special sense by which we detect the presence of the spirits of the dead, as well as the bogies and other evil spirits that abound at night.

My Person and his mate and their young inhabit a very old house that literally teems with spirits, some good and some malignant, and there are a distressing number of bogies who stray onto the property almost every night, particularly when there are no stars and no moon. Some of them ride the wind and hover near the doors and windows, and would come inside if I did not keep a constant alert, warning them away with growling and a show of teeth. Yet it is only on the rarest of occasions that any of my People are aware of them, even when they gibber at the windows and fleer and cry, or shout down the rainspouts. The ghost of the old man who tramps heavily up the front stairs, and the one of the young child who runs through the upstairs hall at night, have been noticed on several occasions by all of my People, but as both of them are quite harmless, I ignore them.

The Dog who wants to get along with his People will warn them only of the presence of the most malignant spirits and bogies and keep quiet about the others that do no harm or, at the worst, are given only to tiresome pranks like door-opening and bookhiding. To do nothing may call for great restraint, but the thoughtful Dog will recognize that few People appreciate having a Dog pace up and down through the house, warning them of every spirit manifestation; they may even put him out when he

would prefer to be in! Dingo, who has all the nervous hyperten-
sions typical of the German Shepherd breed, and who has a quite
unreasonable aversion to spirits, has never learned to hold her
tongue. The silly bitch is consequently ejected from the house
nearly every night and spends many miserable hours in wind and
rain that could better be spent by the den fire.

Just to illustrate how insensitive People can be to the entire
world of spirits, all the time that my special Person has been help-
ing me to write this chapter, a quite harmless spirit—the ghost of
the young lady who wears the long white nightgown—has been
reading over his shoulder, and he never noticed; so I said nothing
about the matter.

WHAT GOOD ARE PEOPLE?

The very title of this chapter is an indictment of our age, an
implicit admission of the materialism that has permeated our
society. One might as well ask, what good are puppies? Must we
analyze, dissect our feelings, apply to all that is inherently beautiful the test of utility, valuing only that which can be shown to be
novel or useful? Must we treasure only the new bone and forget
the old? Our grandsires would have scorned to ask what good are
People, and had they been asked, they would not have deigned an
answer. But theirs was an age of unabashed sentiment, while ours
is one of shamefaced cynicism. So let us dispose of the question
once and for all.

Despite their limitations, which I have suggested in the previ-
ous chapter, People are highly useful to Dogs and well worth all
the trouble and worry that their ownership entails.

I have known several Dogs who had never owned a Person, and
though they extolled their freedom to come and go as they chose,

without the encumbering responsibility of caring for and protecting People, I cannot help but feel that their lives were as empty as their bellies, and that they sensed the futility of their irresponsible existence while they were most vigorously defending it.

One such Person-less Dog comes to mind as a prime example. He was a rather withdrawn, nervous individual of mixed blood, indifferently groomed and given to looking over his shoulder when he talked. As I recall, on one of the few occasions when I managed to draw him out, he told me that his mother was a well-connected Samoyed; he was uncertain about his father, but said that his mother thought he might have been a Dalmation who was visiting in the neighborhood. His very long, strangely spotted coat would tend to bear out his mother's belief, though some of the spots were perhaps grease marks. He lived by himself in an automobile junkyard at the edge of town and sometimes he would piddle onto my farm in search of rabbits, in the catching of which he had a marvelous virtuosity. On several occasions I joined him in the hunt, when I wasn't busy, and shared the kill with him, eating only a few bites out of politeness, for after one has grown accustomed to the Sacred Foods, prepared by People through the mystery of Fire, one loses the taste for wild meat; it will sate the hunger of the body, but it will do nothing to fulfill the soul. But as I was saying, my friend did a lot of bragging about what sport it was to "go wolf" and "camp out" whenever he wanted to and overturn treasure cans and dig in the city dump for food and sleep in a different car every night; but he had a lowtail look about him, just the same, when he heard my Person whistle me home to dinner.

He even bragged that no Person had ever laid a paw on him! I could only think how much he had missed, for a Person's paws—the front ones, I mean—are the most wonderful and mysterious and compelling organs in the world, even more remarkable and significant than our noses.

My earliest puppyhood recollection is not of the touch of my mother's tongue, nor of the milk smell of her nipples, nor of the warmth and security of her belly fur, but of the feel of the paws of my first Person. I could hardly have been more than a day old when I first experienced the inexplicable sense of security that these paws imparted to me. They held me gently yet securely, so that my panic abated and I ceased to struggle against them, and then a single toe began to explore my body with a slow, stroking motion, most novel and delicious, and finally came to the magic, immeasurably sensitive spot behind the ear, where it rubbed and stroked and titillated till every nerve in my body throbbed with rapture, and from that moment I became a People-Owner.

These same paws held me again, a few days later, while something painful was done by a strange Person to my rear end that left it sore for several days. I have since learned that this was the ritual operation of tail-docking by which we Sheepdogs are rid of the absurdly long tails with which we are born, and by which we are rendered different from most other breeds and superior to all.

It was from these same human paws that I received my first taste of Sacred Food—some finely chopped and scraped fragments of rare roast beef. It shames me to admit that, with the perversity of puppyhood, I struggled and gagged and tried to spit it out, not weeping that, having once partaken of the Sacrament, I would be forever different.

My next experience with a Person's paws, which I still vividly recall, took place when I was still very young, for I had not yet shed my milk teeth. I was then living in my first Person's house, and had just finished eating a large and wholly satisfying dish of Sacred Food—as I recall, a soft-boiled egg mixed with finely diced toast and moistened with milk. I urgently needed to go out.

Though I mentioned the matter several times to my Person, she failed to heed me. Not wanting to be overweening or importunate, for I was an unassuming puppy, I found an out-of-the-way corner behind the couch in the living room where the rug was pleasantly grasslike, and barely had begun to relieve myself when one paw delivered a ringing slap on my rump, and then the two paws seized me and ejected me from the house with great suddenness and firmness.

And then there was the morning when I came to join my Special Person, the one with whom I now live. I had been in the wire box for hours and hours, and many strange and indescribable things had happened to me, accompanied by many loud sounds, so that I had gone in the box from where I had always been to a new place, with different smells that were most confusing and, I admit, rather sinister and frightening. And then my Person came and stood before the box, and his smell filled the box, and I knew it was good and right, and his clever paws opened the box and let me out. And he gave me the inside of his paw to smell and taste, and a warmth began to spread through my body and the fear to leave me. And then his paw curled around under my jaw and up the side of my face and came unerringly to rest at the magic Spot just behind my ear, and the toes began to work through the fur of my undercoat and to scratch with excruciatingly delightful expertise, so that I quivered and sighed and laid my weight against his hind leg and took him for my Special Person forever.

What could a Person-less Dog know of such great mysteries?

I know a Dog who owns a Person who cannot see, and whom he leads through the city streets so as to exercise him and keep him content, watching out for him and lending him the keen sight of his own eyes. Yet this Dog's Person is far less dependent upon the Dog's vision than the Dog is upon the magic that resides in his Person's paws, which seem to have a vision of their own and do for him many things that no Dog, however intelligent, can perform for himself.

When you become a Person-Owner, you too will know the magic in your Person's paws. With these paws, he will open doors for you that no scratching can budge. His agile toes will burrow through your coat, find the fat ticks, and destroy them. They will seek out the ticks and fleas, no matter in what inaccessible places they may take refuge, and kill them. The paws will close your cuts when you have been fighting other dogs or have torn yourself on fences, and then comfort and reassure you till the pain is forgotten. They will draw out the thorns from your pads and the burrs from your whiskers. They will spread a soft bed for you in a warm place when you are cold and wet. They will fill your bowl to overflowing with cool water when you are hot and thirsty. And they will prepare the Sacred Food and set it before you for your pleasure and nourishment, several times daily when you are very young, and once daily when you have reached the dignity of Doghood.

Sometimes the paws will smite and chastise you when you have sinned against the rules by which Dogs share their lives with People to their mutual betterment, but you will never profane the rule by biting the paws, no matter how they sting you, for this is the great sin which no People-Owner can commit without incurring the scorn of all self-respecting Dogs.

So, if I must advance arguments for People-Owning based solely upon utility, I rest my case. Just as People are dependent for their safety and welfare upon our senses of smell and hearing, which to them must appear quite magical, so we are equally dependent upon the magic that resides in the paws of People, from which we derive many inexpressible benefits.

Yet when one explores more deeply the spiritual needs of canines, one finds still stronger arguments for People-Owning, arguments that transcend the practical. For it is only through People-Owning that our race is able to experience love in its deepest and purest manifestations. Our own love affairs are transitory things, passing frenzies, physically impelling but spiritually superficial. Our inter-canine relations are limited at best to warm friendships; only with People can we experience selfless, enduring love.

This is the fact that all Dogs, even the most cynical, know in their hearts. This is the ultimate truth of Dogdom. This is what all Dogs remember racially when they are cold, when they are wet, when they are lost, when they cry the moon, when they twitch and whimper in their sleep, and no amount of strutting and tree piddling and high tailing will change it. For there was a time, an eternity of separateness, an eternity without love, before the first wolf-dog took the first human for his own.

CONTENTMENT
AS TOLD TO BURGES JOHNSON

I like the way that the world is made,
   (Tickle me, please, behind the ears)
With part in the sun and part in the shade
   (Tickle me, *please,* behind the ears).
This comfortable spot beneath a tree
Was probably planned for you and me;
Why *do* you suppose God made a flea?
   Tickle me more behind the ears.

I hear a cricket or some such bug
   (Tickle me, please, behind the ears)
And there is a hole some creature dug
   (Tickle me, *please,* behind the ears).
I can't quite smell it from where we sit,
But I think a rabbit would hardly fit;
Tomorrow, perhaps, I'll look into it:
   Tickle me more behind the ears.

A troublesome fly is near my nose,
  (Tickle me, please, behind the ears);
He thinks I'll snap at him, I suppose,
  (Tickle me, *please*, behind the ears).
If I lay on my back with my legs in air
Would you scratch my stomach, just here and there?
It's a puppy trick and I don't much care,
  But tickle me more behind the ears.

Heaven, I guess, is all like this
    (Tickle me, please, behind the ears);
It's my idea of eternal bliss
    (Tickle me, *please*, behind the ears).
With angel cats for a dog to chase,
And a very extensive barking space,
And big bones buried all over the place,—
    And you, to tickle behind my ears.

REMARKS FROM THE PUP
AS TOLD TO BURGES JOHNSON

She's taught me that I mustn't bark
    At little noises after dark,
But just refrain from any fuss
    Until I'm sure they're dangerous.
This would be easier, I've felt,
    If noises could be seen or smelt.

She's very wise, I have no doubt,
    And plans ahead what she's about;
Yet after eating, every day,
    She throws her nicest bones away.
If she were really less obtuse
    She'd bury them for future use.

But that which makes me doubt the most
    Those higher powers that humans boast
Is not so much a fault like that,
    Nor yet her fondness for the cat,
But on our pleasant country strolls
    Her dull indifference to holes!

Ah me! what treasure might be found
  In holes that lead to underground!
However vague or small one is,
  It sends me into ecstasies;
While she, alas! stands by to scoff,
  Or meanly comes to call me off.

Oh, if I once had time to spend
  To reach a hole's extremest end,
I'd grab it fast, without a doubt,
  And promptly pull it inside out;
Then drag it home with all my power
  To chew on in a leisure hour.

Of all the mistresses there are,
  Mine is the loveliest by far!
For would I wag myself apart
  If I could thus reveal my heart.
But on some things, I must conclude,
  Mine is the saner attitude.

THIRTY

BIG DOG THUNDER
BY SAMMY

I'm never scared of dogs I see
So why is it? I wonder,
The only thing that frightens me
Is Big Dog Thunder.

No matter how to hide I try
He tears the place asunder
And blinds me with his flashing eye,
That Big Dog Thunder.

He sees me crouched behind a chair
Or knows which bed I'm under,
I hear him growling everywhere,
That Big Dog Thunder.

But when I'm sitting on your knee,
Though round us he may blunder,
He knows he cannot frighten me,
That Big Dog Thunder.

FROM SPOT: AN AUTOBIOGRAPHY
BY SPOT

BARK THE FIRST
I GO INTO SOCIETY—LOSE MY BALANCE,
AND GAIN A FRIEND.

Every dog has his day. I have had mine, and enjoyed it thoroughly. I come of a good old stock. My father, a wiry-haired
Foxterrier, was a cadet of a well-known Irish family who settled
in England many years ago. There they achieved much distinc-
tion in various walks of life; and my father, who adopted the calling of a baker's dog, was widely known for his fighting, ratting,
and other virtuous qualities. To my mother, a smooth and gentle
creature of humbler origin, I owe the softer graces which have
been my passport to society. Constitutionally averse from those
stormy scenes in which my father eventually lost his valuable life,
I am considered to have inherited from him an excellent appetite,
which I am thankful to say has survived even the loss of my teeth.

My earliest recollections are chiefly of a nice, comfortable basket, well lined with straw, which I and my brothers and sisters,
four in number, used to occupy along with my mother. We
youngsters must then have been about a month old; our tail-
stumps were quite healed, we were in good fettle, and as plump as
quails. Our mother, too, was beginning to feel less anxious about
us. And here I may remark that there never was a better mother
than ours. When I think of the way in which she used sometimes
to go without her food rather than leave us, I am lost in wonder
at the eccentricity of the female character. Having been a father

myself, I can truly aver that I have never once allowed any paternal weakness to interfere with the paramount duty of eating whenever I got the chance.

One day, just about this time, as I happened during an interval of refreshment to be reposing peacefully on my mother's bosom, I was awakened by feeling a strange sensation at the back of my neck. Fancy my surprise on finding myself suspended in mid-air, being carefully regarded the while by a pair of bright, keen, human eyes! Then my mouth was gently opened by fingers of which I rather liked the taste, and my palate inspected. The result of this examination must have been to my credit; for after some talking, which I was then too young to understand, I found myself transferred to a coat pocket of the person who held me; and from that day to this I have never laid eyes again upon my mother or the basket.

Though fond of warmth, and not over partial to ventilation, I found that coat pocket rather stuffy; and was half suffocated, in addition to being most uncomfortably jolted about during my stay therein, which I should think must have lasted over three-quarters of an hour. At length the same hand—I recognised it by the smell—which had consigned me to its depths pulled me forth carefully; and all at once I found myself in the midst of a glare and bustle very trying to a dog of tender age.

"Oh, what a delicious roley-poley!" cried a clear voice that I afterwards grew to love very much. "Why does it sneeze and blink its eyes so?" asked another; and many similar remarks—none of them unkind, though—were made about my personal appearance. Meanwhile, having got over my first discomfort, I sat down on the table where my master had placed me, and began gravely to take stock of my surroundings.

Ours was a nice room, with a comfortable smell. There were

lots of places in it where a dog could make himself very snug. If it had a fault, it was that it was rather too clean and overstocked with flowers. I never cared for flowers, finding their odour sickly. How vapid is the scent of a rose, for instance, compared with that of an old, seasoned bone!

As for those dear, kind friends who stood around me, how shall I describe them? It did a pup's heart good to look at their pleasant faces and listen to their cheery voices; so that my bit of a tail must needs set itself to wag involuntarily, whereat they all began to laugh afresh.

There was Agnes, who had first spoken, a tall girl, fair to look upon—at least I think so; just the sort of girl who might be trusted to share her last morsel with a dog. My heart warmed to her at once, and has never cooled from that day to this. Even now, at the mere thought of her, my tail begins to wobble.

There were Bob and Charlie, two small boys of an exceedingly pleasant smell. Oh, what games I have had with them! Both were nice, but I liked Bob the better of the two: his hands were not so clean as Charlie's, and there was more fun in his eyes.

There was my Master—that great and good being, wisest and mightiest of all the men on earth! In appearance he seemed slightly younger than Agnes, but with more of determination about the eyes and mouth. The beauty and majesty of his person were beyond all description.

On a sofa near the fire reclined an elderly lady, watching what went on, with an amused expression on her pale and worn face. Agnes carried me over to the sofa and placed me on the old lady's lap. She patted me a little, saying I was nice and plump; but did not give me the idea then of caring much for dogs, though we became very good friends on the whole. In that part of the room there was an odour which I afterwards noticed in the village apothecary's shop, and which I at first disliked very much; though having grown accustomed to it and somewhat attached to the old lady, I used to frequent the sofa a good deal. There was a capital place under it for sheltering in when one got into disgrace; also for the concealment of bones and other valuable possessions which, by the way, always disappeared by the next morning, leaving no trace behind except their smell.

Upon the hearthrug lay a big black cat, who did not appear to take the least notice of what was going on, though, as I soon found out, nothing escaped her. I never could abide cats, they are so mean and underhand. Morality demands their extermination, and I have always shown myself their unsparing enemy. An exception had to be made in favour of one's house-cat— more's the pity!

During the whole time that I sat on the table, making what I could out of my novel surroundings, an animated discussion was going on as to the properest name for me. A great many queer names were suggested, especially by the boys, but none of them seemed to give general satisfaction. At length my dear Agnes, who always did the right thing, said in her quiet way: "I really don't think; we can do better than to call him Spot. It is an easy name, and that brown mark just over his eye entitles him to it."

"There is but one objection to the name," observed my master, "which is that at least half the fox-terriers in England are so called; consequently, if he is ever lost, it won't be of much use to advertise for a dog that answers to 'Spot.' However, it doesn't matter for the present; call him what you please, until we have had time to think of some better name for him."

Accordingly, "Spot" I became; and "Spot" I remained thenceforth—all of us growing so used to the name that to alter it would have been quite out of the question.

Then they gave me some milk in which to drink my own "Health, and long life" to me! And here I may remark that the milk in that house was always uncommonly good. I have never tasted better, though it has often been my lot to put up with very much worse.

This important ceremony concluded, my dear Agnes took me to her neck and cuddled me, whilst I licked her soft white throat to show my gratitude; though I question if she liked my doing so, for she speedily put me down upon the hearthrug. Then the young people went away, leaving me alone with the old lady and the cat.

I tottered over to the latter, not being very strong on my legs just yet; and, by way of opening a conversation agreeably, intimated as well as I could that I didn't think much of her.

Without moving in the least, she regarded me contemptuously through eyes reduced to mere slits until I had concluded my remarks. Then, in the silent language, she lazily inquired—

"Did you bark?"

"I should think I did, you great stupid!" was my hot reply.

"Oh! if you call *that* barking, I've no more to say," she rejoined, with a provoking grin; "but, if I were you, *I* shouldn't try to bark again until I had learned how."

It was not so much what she said as her way of saying it that provoked me to charge at her, which I did incontinently; but was received with a sharp tap on the nose that stung and disconcerted me very much.

"Keep your distance, my young friend," she said, regarding me sternly, "or you may have to regret the premature loss of your sight. Now, take my advice; sit down there quietly, and behave like a rational being—that is, *if you can.*"

Involuntarily I obeyed her, for the tap on my nose had puzzled me considerably. You see I was then very young indeed, and it was my first experience of claws.

She continued to survey me quietly for some time; and then, still using the silent language, she resumed the conversation, as follows:

"So *you* are the new dog they have been wishing for ever since old Bruno's death; just as if a cat was not good enough for them? Well, I give them joy of their bargain. Bruno was a fool; but, may I never taste milk again! if he looked half such a fool as you."

This was hard to bear; but I bore it, not having yet fully recovered from my surprise. Getting no answer, she appeared to dismiss me from her attention altogether, and began to make her toilet. I watched the process for some time with great curiosity, wondering how she managed to lick herself in such out-of-the-way places. At last, feeling that I must speak or burst—

"How is it," I asked, impetuously, "that you contrive to stretch out your hind-leg so far while you are licking the back of it?"

"Never mind my legs," she retorted; "it is extremely indelicate of you to allude to them: no gentledog would."

"It is far more indelicate of you to make such a display of them," I blurted out, for her manner enraged me.

She paused in her licking immediately, and regarded me for a moment with a cold and steady, but not unfriendly, gaze.

"Well," she remarked, "I didn't think you had it in you. For a raw young pup, that was really smart. Now, if you have no objection, as I have finished dressing, I'll put you up to the ways of the place; and after that, whether we shall be friends or not depends upon yourself."

This at least was civil; and I signified my assent by stretching myself upon the rug in front of her, with my nose between my two fore-paws, whilst she, squatting down with all her feet under her in the way that cats do, proceeded to enlighten me as she had promised.

"You may consider yourself fortunate," she resumed, still in the silent language—she seldom used any other, except at night—"in having your lot cast here. The house is a comfortable one, and they keep up good fires. There's no stint of food, and no dog on the premises but yourself."

"The people, too, seem very nice," I put in.

"Oh, *they* are of small importance," she retorted, snappishly, "compared with what I am speaking of. Not that I have much fault to find with them," she added reflectively, "except that the boys are inconsiderate. The old woman's the best of the lot."

"Is she?" said I. "*I* like the one they call 'Agnes' better."

"That is because you are young and silly," she replied. "The old woman is very fond of *me;* whereas Agnes simply does her duty by me—nothing more. I know as well as how I am sitting on this rug that all her affection is given to her mother and brothers, and to a silly young man who comes loafing in here at times, and whom it is my opinion she is in love with."

"What do you mean by that?" I asked.

"Oh, I forgot that puppies don't understand what love means," she remarked, with a demure simper. "Perhaps I was wrong to say so much when I have only suspicion to go upon. Indeed, now that I think of it, she has never once been out on the tiles with him that I can remember. So, if you please, Mr. Pup, we'll forget all that has escaped me on that subject."

I eyed her with intense disfavour as she sat there blinking and trying to look virtuous. After a pause, I inquired—

"And my master, what do you think of *him?*"

"Your master," she said deliberately, "is one of the most

insufferably conceited young prigs that it has ever been my lot to encounter."

Of course, I did not wait to hear more; but charged her with all the noise and violence of which I was capable. She was quite taken aback by this sudden onset, for cats are easily frightened, though slow to give in; and, springing to her feet, arched her back and spat at me like a fury.

"You wretched, unmannerly, little vagabond!" she hissed; "how dare you use such language to a lady, and try to bite her legs when she is off her guard?"

"And how dare *you* speak in such a way of my master, you great trolloping, green-eyed, old vixen? I'll give you something to lick yourself for," I retorted, making another dash at her.

"Hish, hish!" cried the old lady, from the sofa, whom I suppose we had disturbed by our noise; but, as we paid no heed to her remonstrances, she stretched over to the fireplace and caused a bell to ring violently downstairs. Shortly afterwards, a fat woman entered the room.

"Hannah," said the old lady, "take away that little brute, he is beginning to quarrel with Rosa already, and I suppose we shall have no peace now. Oh, dear me! my poor head!"

Hannah made no reply, but, taking me up in one of her big red hands, marched out of the room. A delightful smell of roast meat pervaded this woman's attire; otherwise, she was not attractive.

"Now, just you lie quiet there, or it will be worse for you!" said she, flinging me down upon a mat. "As if there wasn't enough for me to do already, I'm to be groom-o'-the-chambers to a measly pup, am I?" and muttering wrathfully, she resumed her occupation of basting a joint that revolved slowly before a great fire.

The apartment in which I now found myself was perfectly sumptuous. I shall not attempt to describe its manifold attractions;

but shall content myself with saying that everything in it breathed a delightful aroma of food in endless variety.

Unable to remain still, I soon began to explore this region of enchantment. At every step new beauties and lurking odours revealed themselves to my enthralled senses. Anon, my devious footsteps led me to a sort of cave under what, I now know, was the kitchen dresser.

Entering it, I threaded my way amid sombre pots and saucepans, which exhaled the subtlest odours, till suddenly I found my way barred by a mighty obstacle extending across the whole depth of the cavern. To surmount this now became my object. By the most strenuous exertions I just managed to get the upper part of my body over its edge. Well would it have been for me if I had paused there, but youthful ambition urged me on! I struggled vigorously with every limb; and, losing my balance, toppled right over with a splash into briny depths below.

"Drat the little beast, if he ain't got into the fishkettle!" exclaimed the fat woman as, rushing over, she extricated me from what might have proved a salt-watery grave. "Well, I hope you're satisfied now," she continued, while roughly drying me with a dish-clout. "It 'ud ha' been a mussy to us all if I hadn't heard ye splashing—that it would. We could have spared ye very well, ye little devil. Now, go out in the sun and dry yourself." So saying, she carried me into the back garden, where she deposited me on a grass plot.

I felt very down in the mouth then, I can tell you. My coat was sticky and uncomfortable, and my eyes smarted considerably from the salt in them. To add to my discomfiture, a few yards off was seated my old enemy, the cat, laughing as if she would split.

"My word!" jeered the odious creature, "but you *do* look a guy! Been up to some mischief, I expect, and had not the sense to get out of it, as the merest kitten would. Oh yes! dogs are superior animals, sure*ly!*"

I had not the spirit to answer her, but sat shivering and down-hearted while she continued to ply me with sarcasm at her leisure; when suddenly relief came to me from an unexpected quarter. The garden gate flew open with a bang. There was a rush and a scurry along the gravel walk; whereupon my enemy, suddenly decamping climbed with great agility into an adjacent tree.

"Come down out of that, you nasty black catamaran! Come down here, and I'll tear you to bits!" shouted a great, powerfully-built dog, who was gesticulating wildly at the foot of the tree. "Come down here, I say!"

"Thank you, I feel perfectly comfortable where I am," replied the cat, looking down at him from a fork of the tree where she was now securely seated. "Pray, don't worry yourself on *my* account. You are the butcher's dog, aren't you? I perceive your master's cart outside, and I hope he has not forgotten to bring my lights."

"Bother your lights! I wish they may choke you," he retorted, still making frantic, but useless, efforts to reach her. "What an infernal row you and that sneaking old Tom, whom you are carrying on with, made last night! I could scarcely get a wink of sleep."

"If you are referring to the serenade with which my friend at the Rectory was good enough to entertain me, you show a signal want of musical taste," she replied with much *hauteur*. "He has, simply, the most lovely voice I ever heard; and, though it is not for me to say it," she added, mincingly, "I have heard a good many."

"I've no doubt you have, you old Jezebel!" he returned, "for, of all the cats in the parish, you bear the worst reputation; but, if I ever come across your elderly warbler, I'll spoil his music for him, that I will!"

Having thus relieved his mind, my deliverer turned, panting from his exertions, to where I sat contemplating the scene with much interest. Soon his whole demeanour underwent a pleasing change, for most dogs are good to young folk. Standing well over me, he surveyed me attentively for a while, his legs wide apart, his ears cocked, and his tail vibrating amicably. Then in the silent language addressed me encouragingly—

"Cheer up, youngster! Any good smells hereabouts?"

Flattered by his condescension, I hastened to inform him with becoming modesty that, being only a new arrival, I was not in a position to answer the question. Whereupon he suggested that we should explore the premises together.

We sauntered round by the back of the house, passing few smells of any importance until we arrived at the ashpit, which at once struck me as possessing high olfactory merit; and I said as much.

"Yes" he admitted, dubiously; "there is plenty of it, certainly; but rather too mixed for *me*. However it's all a matter of choice: *you* prefer a blend, *I* like my smells plain and pungent. Hallo! what have we here?"

Saying this, he fished out a large bone from a heap of kitchen refuse, and set to work upon it without more ado.

Now there is no dog, however young and anxious to please, who would like to see a bone that properly belongs to himself appropriated in such a fashion; so I at once proceeded to inform him that he was dealing with my property.

"Nonsense!" he replied, gruffly. "This is a case of *seniores priores.*"

"What's that?" I asked, struck by the novelty of the expression.

"Dog-Latin," was the curt rejoinder.

I'M THE DOG
AS TOLD TO GRENVILLE KLEISER

I'm the dog
They drag along
Dust-strewn streets,
Thru jostling throng.

I'm the dog
All chocolate-fed;
Wonder is
I'm not dead.

I'm the dog
They hourly praise
With honeyed words
My tricks and ways.

I'm the dog
They worry so;
Tho often tired
I have to go.

I'm the dog
They pet all day;
From talking bores
Relief I pray.

I'm the dog
That likes night best;
When they're asleep,
I get some rest!

FROM THE DOG
BY SCAMP
AS TOLD TO G.E. MITTON

'Whatever he is, he's beautiful,' she said.
'You're just silly about that dog!'
'I shall be as silly as I like.'
'You spoil him.'
'Indeed I don't.'
This was true; dearly as she loved me, that tender, loyal mistress of mine, her treatment was strict. Many and many a time has she used a stinging switch to my sides with all the force of her vigorous young arm. At such times I lay still, of course. There are one or two things in me that must have been inherited from good dogs and true. For one thing, there was no punishment she could give me that I could not take without crying out. She never had to hold me; I just lay there as still as a stone until she had done. Once it was very bad. I had been out for a ramble in the fields by myself, and I came upon a lot of little lambs dancing and skipping in a field, and my blood danced in me. There was a smell about them that made me want to roll them over and worry at them, half in play, but with some force too. In an instant I was in among them, and had caught the silly things, and rolled them over, and worried at them. I did not hurt them, their woolly hair was too thick for that, and I was young, but I was just drunk— with the sheer joy of it. Then—oh then, quite suddenly in the middle of it all I heard her voice, 'Scamp!' and my heart nearly leaped out of my body, for I knew quite well how awfully wrong it was. She came across the field and I lay down, and she flogged me hard, and then sent me flying home before her in disgrace to

the stables. I ran straight upstairs to the hayloft where I slept at that time, for I knew she would lock me up. When she came after me I crouched in the darkest corner and went thump, thump with my tail on the floor to see if she'd let me be sorry yet, but she would not. She just turned the key in the lock and went away. It was hours before she came again. I knew the very minute she opened the door downstairs; then she came up step by step, and as she opened the door in that dusky place she said, 'Is he sorry?' I crawled out, dragging myself along low down, and she came and sat down in the hay, and put her arms around me, and said, 'Oh, darling, it was very very naughty to play with the little lambs; they didn't understand, and nearly died of fright. Never do it again. Good dog now.'

Then I wriggled and waggled and tried to kiss her face, until she laughed outright and told me I was quite quite good, and we both danced all the way to the house.

One of the first things she had taught me after 'fetch' was perfect obedience. When I was quite a puppy, and had done anything naughty, I would not come to be whipped; I used to sit down just out of reach, and by wriggling violently try to insinuate that now the time for 'quite quite good' had come; and when she came near me I would go a little farther, and so on. Now I must explain that our house had two staircases, and the length of the house both upstairs and down ran a passage, so that one could go all round. When I was in this puppy mood, I would run half-way up the stairs, and put my head between the balusters and smile at her, and when she came up I would go along the passage and so down the back stairs, and along the passage and up the front stairs again, always waiting until she got in sight before I went a little farther; but the annoying part was that when I came upstairs again some one had always shut the passage door, so I couldn't get on and had to crouch down and listen with a beating heart to her steps coming nearer and nearer. In this way she always caught me, and I learned at last that it was no use running away, I must come at once when she called me; and when I did sometimes she only talked to me very seriously, and let me off with the beating.

All these are very little things, but I was only a little dog then, and big things didn't happen to me. But I look back on my happy school-days, when she and I were all the world to each other, with such pleasure that I cannot help being rather prosy over them.

One thing we had a difference of opinion about, and that was cats. I think she rather liked them; well, so did I, though not quite in the same way.

I think a world without cats would have been a much less interesting world, for one would miss the unexpectedness of cats, who were constantly turning up in places quite near the house where one couldn't hope to find a rabbit or anything better to chivvy. I never chivvied the house cat, Tiger, for he and I were friends, and understood one another, though we sometimes pretended to be enemies just for the fun of it, and flew round and round the lawns, he with his tail up and his fur standing out, and I snapping and snarling, until he suddenly turned round and became a tame cat again, and I lay down an ordinary panting little dog. But I did love to run down other cats, and there were no end of them, though they weren't always to be got at. I have tried to tire out a cat in a tree by watching it with a disinterested air, hoping it would think I was harmless and come down; but it always seemed to prefer to be exactly where it was, even on the thinnest little bough, and its expression of 'wouldn't change my position if you offered me a throne' was very exasperating. This sometimes took me in, so I went for a drink; but when I came back it had always gone, so I knew it was all humbug, and it had really been most uncomfortable; cats are the slyest creatures, they never play fair. But the real glorious fun was to chase one when there were no trees about, and see him running for his life, and perhaps get him into a corner and go for him. All the spittings and scratchings added to the excitement, though I must say that afterwards my nose was sometimes very sore. I never killed a cat quite by myself; it's a very difficult thing to do, because another mean trick they have is never to face the same way for two seconds together; they just seem to shimmer, so that all the front of them is face and claws, and you can't get in. Nip helped me once, and together we got through the shimmery face and into the real cat at the back. I was rather glad afterwards when it was all over that my mistress did not know, though I think she suspected, but she imagined Nip was the real sinner. I'll tell you about Nip in another chapter. She was my first dog friend.

Yes, cat-chivvying is just grand, and the football scrimmages that men are so fond of are not in it for excitement; but, do you know, I grew so fond of Gill that at last if she shouted 'Lie down,' I would drop, even if I were almost touching a cat that was flying for its life.

She wasn't stern all the time; we used to have grand romps in the winter evenings. Hide-and-seek all over the house, when I lay trembling with excitement in the hall, and she hid upstairs and gave the wee-est whistle; but I could always smell her out. I've been blessed with a very good nose, and afterwards, as you shall hear, that power of smell did me some good turns and one or two bad ones. Then she would hide a handkerchief in the dining-room under cushions or down the backs of chairs, and I would come to look for it, standing on my hind legs to peep on the table, and sniffing under the cushions, and then when I found it what laughter and chasings we had.

FROM INTO HIS OWN
AS TOLD TO CLARENCE KELLAND

The Airedale narrating this story is an orphan lost in a fire as a puppy. He fends for himself in the city, and develops a feud with a champion bull terrier, Joggs. The Airdale catches Joggs attacking sheep; the two dogs fight and are interrupted by Joggs' owner...

SANDY KENS A DOG WHEN HE SEES ONE

The man with the Airedale talk came to me and patted me and I licked his hand. He took my muzzle and looked into my face and shook his head. Then he straightened me up and eyed me all over and sucked in his breath.

"Somethin' is no as it should be here," says he to himself. "Yon's no tramp dog stock."

From me the man went to Joggs, who was just beginning to crawl about.

"What's this?" says he. "Come take a look."

He was holding Joggs' mouth open.

"Look ye," says he, pointing in. "Tell me, is that no sheep's wool? Eh, man?"

The other man looked and frowned and seemed upset.

"'Tis caircumstantial eevidence," says my friend, "but we'll gie the accused anither test. Do you go and admeenister a kick to yon sheep."

The man did as he was told, and at sight of it I couldn't keep still. I growled and started for him.

"Nay, laddie, nay," says my friend, grabbing me quick. "Ye

could no see the sheep abused, could ye? Now what think ye, Mister Hollands?"

The other man didn't say anything, but just stood thinking. While he stood Joggs stood up, and at that I walked to the hurt sheep and stood over it with my hair bristling, daring Joggs to come on.

"Look ye there," says my friend. "Does that no tell which is sheep-killin' and which is no?"

I guess there wasn't any doubting who was guilty. I know what was left of Joggs looked guilty enough. His master scowled at him.

"If he wasn't worth more money than the whole flock of sheep I'd give him a charge of shot," he said, angry-like.

"How aboot this ither laddie?" says my friend. "I'd like well tae see him clean, Mister Hollands. 'Tis Airedale he is, sir, wi' no blemish in his blood, or I'm a Sassenach."

The other man's eyes began to twinkle. "He gave Joggs a licking. Any dog that can do that is worth his feed."

"Thank ye, sir," said my friend, and then he turned to me. "Will ye come wi' me, laddie? Eh?" I wagged my tail and followed him. Both of them carried Joggs, who was too weak to walk.

My friend, whose name turned out to be Sandy, washed me up and put stuff on my cuts and fixed up a place for me to lie down in the stable. I wasn't sorry to take a long sleep. When I woke up again I felt as good as ever, barring a little smarting where Joggs' teeth had been gnawing around. So I walked out into the yard to look for Sandy and something to eat.

Mr. Hollands hadn't many dogs; just a couple of setters and Joggs and a fox terrier by the name of Scoot. But every one was a thoroughbred and every one had brought home ribbons from bench shows. I was the only one that couldn't brag about my pedigree—and I could, but there was no way of proving it.

However, the other dogs besides Joggs were pleasant and friendly. It tickled them to see Joggs get thrashed, and they told me so. But, kind as they were, they made me feel somehow that I was different. What with their talk about pedigrees and their recollections of what happened at this bench show and that bench show, I was sort of out of it. They were always talking blue ribbons and cups and things like that, when I didn't so much as have a tin plate.

I learned that the next show came along in November and ended so the dogs would get home for Thanksgiving. That was quite a while off, so it didn't bother me any, and besides it was none of my business, for I wouldn't go. Folks don't pay entry fees for stray dogs as a general thing.

Sandy was proud of me. You wouldn't believe it, but he was fonder of me than of any of the rest. Once I heard him bragging about me to Mr. Hollands and showing my points.

"Ye canna fool me aboot Airedales," says he. "Did I no see Ayreshire Lass and Argyle Champion morn, noon and night for a matter o' a year? 'Twas in the Douglas kennels. An' I'm tellin' ye, sir, this bit doggie no has to take the dust o' anny one o' them."

"Shucks," says Mr. Hollands. "He's only a tramp dog. You're partial to him because he licked Joggs."

"I ken a dog when I see him," says Sandy, stubbornly.

Another time a strange man, walking through the yard with Mr. Hollands, stopped and looked at me.

"Didn't know you went in for Airedales, Hollands," he said.

"I don't," says Mr. Hollands. "That's nothing but a tramp that Sandy picked up."

The strange man looked at me and then called me over to pet me and feel of my back and legs.

"This is your day for joking, isn't it?" he says to Mr. Hollands.

"If this is a tramp, then I'm going to sell every blooded dog in my kennels. Come, now, where did you pick him up? Has he ever been shown?"

"I'm not joking. He's Sandy's and he's a tramp."

"Um," says the man. "Let's see if Sandy'll sell him."

But Sandy wouldn't sell me, though the man argued with him half an hour. Finally the stranger told Sandy he didn't blame him and asked if he was going to send me to the show. Sandy said he never thought of it, and couldn't see much use.

"Tell you what I'll do," said the stranger. "I'll back my judgment of that dog. You send him and I'll pay his fee and expenses. How's that, Sandy?"

"Tis a bargain," says Sandy.

And that's how I came to be entered in the show.

It tickled me, though I hadn't any idea I'd have any luck, but I knew it would please Mother if she could hear of it. I hadn't forgotten her, you'd better believe, and was just as determined as ever to find her. I hadn't forgotten old Pete either, but he was timid about coming around. The best I could do for him was to hide out bones where he would find them. But he was a born tramp, and it was hard for him to stay in one place. Finally he told me he was going to take to the road and we said good-bye. And I've never seen him again. I wish I might, now, for I'd like to tell him what a lot I owe him.

All this time Joggs had been kept shut up where he couldn't get at the sheep and where he and I couldn't get at each other. He didn't have any sense. There's such a thing as courage and there's such a thing as foolishness—which was what Joggs had. He would have fought a freight engine, and if I'd licked him every day for a month, he would have come the next day for another licking.

It was getting pretty cold now, and November was commencing. Nothing was talked of by the dogs but the show and the Thanksgiving that followed. Mr. Hollands always celebrated Thanksgiving by having a lot of folks out from the city, and he celebrated for his dogs, too, especially if they did well at the show.

During that month we had especial care—even myself, for Sandy kept getting prouder and prouder of me every day. At last he got so he believed I was the equal of Argyle Champion, that he used to know, and he said he bet my mother was as good a dog as Ayreshire Lass. But I knew that was all bosh.

Going to the show was no fun. Riding in the train upset my stomach, and I was pretty glad to get out and go to the big hall where the show was, even if I did have to be tied in a sort of stall with dogs on all sides of me that kept barking and yelping and disturbing me. There was every sort of dog in the world. Right where I was, though, there were nothing but Airedales, and I never imagined there were so many of us.

Over at my right I could see a square place where men kept leading dogs and other men looked at them and poked them and felt them and wrote in little books. The dog next to me said that was where the judging was done and that those men were the judges. That made me sort of excited and nervous, though, as I have said, I knew there would be no ribbons for me.

THE TITLE IS HANDED DOWN

It was two days before the Airedales were reached. Sandy had fussed around me like an old hen—you know how they act when they have chicks. He washed me and combed me until I was actually sore. I saw dog after dog go past and get examined. I was pretty nearly the last one.

"It's just a formality, Sandy," says Mr. Hollands. "Argyle Champion will hold his honors. But as long as your dog is entered, you might as well have him looked over."

Sandy's jaw was set, but he didn't say a word as he led me through the gate.

The judges were standing around careless-like when I came in, but when Sandy lifted me up on the stand they seemed to get interested, and asked Sandy all sorts of questions. Then they went over me careful. You never saw anybody take such pains as they did to see what there was to me. Finally a big man with a badge shook his head and said it was beyond him, and that such things didn't happen.

"Set the champion up here," says he, and Argyle Champion was put by my side. We didn't look at each other. I didn't dare look at him, he was such an important dog. Imagine being the best Airedale in the United States!

The judges compared us and talked about us, and I could see Sandy chewing on his moustache and almost jumping up and down with excitement.

Well, sir, right in the middle of it I looked over to one side and there stood a dog—an Airedale. For a moment I couldn't believe my eyes, and then I let out a yelp of joy and jumped for her. Men tried to stop me, but I dodged them.

"Mother," I said. "Mother, it's me! It's me!"

She knew me in a second, and if you ever saw two dogs acting happy and glad to see each other, we were those dogs. A man tried to haul me away, but Mother growled at him, and they let us alone and watched us with such surpised looks! We could hear them talking.

"Now, what d'you make of that?" says one.

"It beats me," says another.

"They know each other as sure as shooting," says the big man with the badge.

"Wouldn't it—wouldn't it beat the Dutch," says another man, as if he didn't quite dare say it, "if this was the lost puppy—the one that got out the night of the Douglas Kennels fire?"

"Such things don't happen," says another man.

"Is Weaver here?" says the big man. "He might have some way of recognizing this dog—if it was that puppy. It's our duty to find out if we can. Yes, sir; it's our duty."

In a few minutes they came back with a man they called Weaver, and he was the man who used to come to see Mother and the rest of us so often in the kennels. He was excited, and Mother was excited, and I was excited. Mother ran to him, and then back to me, and licked my face, and then ran back to Weaver. He blinked his eyes as if something was the matter with him.

"If," says Mr. Weaver, "if this is Ayreshire Lass's lost puppy he's got the mark of a scar nicked across his left hind leg a couple of inches above his paw. Jumped on the sharp edge of a tin can, and we were afraid at first it had got the tendon."

The whole crowd of men came for me and lifted me on the stand beside Argyle Champion again, and looked at my leg. I knew what they'd find. I knew there was a little mark across the leg where no hair grew—it was some sort of a scar.

They found it, and—well, sir—they yelled, actually cheered, and Sandy came pushing through them and grabbed me and hugged me, and other folks came crowding around to see what had happened. I never saw such goings-on.

After a while the big man pushed everybody away and says:

"We've got to finish this job," so once more the judges compared me and Argyle Champion inch by inch. Finally the big man turned away and said grufflike:

"There's a new champion, boys."

I didn't understand until I saw Sandy go crazy, and until Mother yelped, and until Argyle Champion, like a real Scotch gentleman, turned his head slowly and looked at me, and said in a voice that was kind, but very, very dignified:

"I congratulate you... It is not an ill thing to be succeeded by one's son—for you are my son, you know."

That's about all. All, except that Mr. Hollands paid a whopping price for my Mother, and sold Joggs—or Raynsford Champion—for another whopping price. Said he wanted no more to do with bulldogs. Then Mother and the rest of the dogs and myself went home.

Next day was Thanksgiving. Maybe you think that is a day just for men and women, but don't fool yourself. Dogs have as much right to give thanks as anybody. We did. I never understood much about Thanksgiving before, but I do now—for Mother and I are together again, and I'm not a tramp for everybody to throw stones at, but am Clydesdale Champion—that's my new kennel name. Yes, I'm thankful—thankful there was a scar on my leg. Why, I have so many things to be thankful for that I can't think of them all.

Which is a pretty good way to be, isn't it?

FED UP
AS TOLD TO JOE WALKER

Yes, it was fun at first to sit and yell
At other dogs and feel an awful swell,
And when I tired of that, then I could creep
Into the back and loll or fall asleep.
Yes, jolly fun—though often when we tore
Faster than usual my left eye felt sore.
Those were the times we used to bump.
  What Ho!
(Scared? Just a bit. I never let them know.)
Oh, it was larks—at first, but now I say
"Bother the thing!" It's Car, Car, Car, all day.
He's always out with it, or, if he's not,
He's underneath and getting cross and hot.
I'd like to help, but if I go and look
He's most ungrateful—"Hi, Dog! Sling
  your hook!"
Whilst as for walks—I shouldn't think I've had
A decent one for weeks, it is too bad!
Crawls to the post and back are all I get,
And even then—The Car! if it looks wet!

I'm off my grub, I'm getting horrid fat,
Don't feel inclined to chase the next-door cat.
I'm fed up! Yes, if I should never see
The smelly beast again—. They're off! HI!
WAIT FOR ME!

FROM A DOG DAY
AS TOLD TO WALTER EMANUEL

1:30	A windfall. A whole dish of mayonaise fish on the slab in the hall. Before you can say Jack Robinson I have bolted it.
1:32	Curious pains in my underneath.
1:33	Pains in my underneath get worse.
1:34	Horrid feeling of sickness.
1:35	Rush up into Aunt Brown's room, and am sick there.
1:37	Better. Think I shall pull through if I am careful.
1:40	Almost well again.
1:41	Quite well again. Thank Heavens! It was a narrow shave that time. People ought not to leave such stuff about.
1:42	Up into dining-room. And, to show how well I am, I gallumph round and round the room, at full pelt, about twenty times, steering myself by my tail. Then, as a grand finale, I jump twice on to the waistcoat-part of old Mr. Brown, who is sleeping peacefully in the arm-chair. He wakes up very angry indeed, and uses words I have never heard before. Even Miss Brown, to my no little surprise, says it is very naughty of me. Old Mr. Brown insists on my being punished, and orders Miss Brown to beat me. Miss Brown runs the burglar for all he is worth. But no good. Old Mr. Brown is dead to all decent feeling! So Miss Brown beats me. Very nice. Thoroughly enjoyable. Just like

being patted. But, of course, I yelp, and pretend it hurts frightfully, and do the sad-eye business, and she soon leaves off and takes me into the next room and gives me six pieces of sugar! Good business. Must remember always to do this. Before leaving she kisses me and explains that I should not have jumped on poor Pa, as he is the man who goes to the City to earn bones for me. Something in that, perhaps. Nice girl.

2:00–3:15 Attempt to kill fur rug in back room.
           No good.
3:45   Sulked.
3:46   Small boy comes in, and strokes me. I snap at him.
           I will not be every one's plaything.
3:47–4:00 Another attempt to kill rug. Would have done it this
           time, had not that odious Aunt Brown come in and
           interfered. I did not say anything, but gave her such
           a look, as much as to say, "I'll do for you one day." I
           think she understood.
4:00–5:15 Slept.

ONLY A DOG
AS TOLD TO GRENVILLE KLEISER

I'm only a dog,—
Not much, you say?
But I have great sport,
I play all day.

I'm only a dog,—
You're sorry for me?
I sleep well at night,
From worry I'm free.

I'm only a dog,—
Sad lot, do you think?
I've good things to eat,
And plenty to drink.

I'm only a dog,—
When I see men at strife,
I'm thankful to God
I lead a dog's life!

pete s holiday
BY PETE THE PUP
AS TOLD TO DON MARQUIS

we found a hill all green with grass
and cool with clover bloom
where bees go booming as they pass
boom zoom boom

my master took me in the car
and high upon the hill
we lay and stared up at the clouds
until the day grew chill

and moths came floating from the sky
and shadows stroked the ground
and we lay still and stared and stared
and what do you think we found

we found a star between the clouds
upon the edge of night
but when i jumped and barked at it
it hid itself in fright

then we drove back to town again
with my head on his lap
it tires a dog to scare a star
and then he needs a nap

my master is the same as god
when he thumps his hand
people bring us hamburg steaks
at any eating stand

o master let us go right now
and find another star
and eat another hamburg steak
at a refreshment bar

FROM LUCKY DOG
BY BOBBIE
AS TOLD TO IAN HAY

"I wonder if he remembers the place where he came from, wher-ever it was," said Harry one day.

"I hope not," said Kit, and turned to me. "You don't remember that horrible place any more, do you, my lovely?"

As a matter of fact, I don't. I have a vague recollection of being pretty cold and hungry long ago, and if anybody moves his foot quickly in my direction I jump back and squeal, for no reason at all; but it all seems to belong to some former existence. My present one does not give me much time for reflection.

Perhaps you would like to hear something about that.

We start the day by being called at nine. That means that Esther, the maid, brings up a cup of tea and some sweet biscuits, and puts them beside my Lady's bed. I get out of my basket and jump on to the bed. (Harry, I may say, has entirely disappeared by this time: he hardly troubles us at all except in the evening.) If my Lady fails to note my arrival, I blow gently into her ear. This awakens her sufficiently to cause her to reach out a hand and give me a biscuit. After that we go to sleep again until ten o'clock, when Esther arrives with a fresh cup of tea and takes away the cold one. Sometimes we sit up and drink this cup, but more often we sleep quietly on, as good as gold, until the eleven o'clock one arrives. After that we get up and dress.

Before lunch we go shopping. There are two kinds of shops—those with counters and those without. Shops with counters are usually dull, unless one can find one's way round to the back, which is not always feasible. Bakers' and provision shops are not so bad, though: I am tolerably well known at most of these now, and my methods are understood. I stand on my hind legs, with my fore-paws against the counter, and bark once. That is usually good for a bun, or a bit of meat.

The first time I entered a provision shop—it was the kind of place where they sell bacon and butter and cheese—I created a sensation by taking one look round and bolting out with my tail between my legs. (Of course this was a very long time ago—quite three months.) The young men behind the counter were much amused, and asked if their faces were as fearful as all that. My Lady, who always understands my reactions, explained that it was probably because I had mistaken them for a row of vets. on account of their white jackets. I may say that we see a good many vets., my Lady being quite unreasonably concerned for my health; and vets., though frequently efficient, are seldom sympathetic when you are left alone with them.

But for real fun commend me to shops without counters, where one can really explore. Quite the best of these is Antoinette's, where my Lady gets her frocks. Antoinette himself I do not like at all: he is rather sleek, like a tomcat, and smells of scent. But his shop is lovely. There are no counters at all—merely wardrobes and glass cases. At one end is an archway screened by curtains, behind which I usually find a number of charming girls, in a considerable state of undress. Naturally I do not allow this to embarrass me; in fact, I frequently stay and share their lunch. After all, one is a man of the world or one is not.

Our great time is in the afternoon, for then my Lady and I go to the Park and play with my ball. It is a very simple game: she throws the ball and I run after it and bring it back. We must do this very well, because we usually attract a number of spectators— mostly small children, who leave their nannies and run across the grass and watch us, breathlessly. After a while they ask if they may join in the game, and this suits everybody—me, because you cannot have too many people to throw balls for you; the nannies, because it gives them a chance to get into the shade and tell each other stories; and my Lady, because she can now play with as many children as she wants—and she wants a lot. They ask her questions. A great many of these are about me, of course—what breed of dog I am, and why parts of me are white and others black, and why one of my ears stands up and the other lies down, and why my forehead bulges so; and she answers them all, and explains how rare it is to find a dog like me at all

After that she generally asks me to do one of my tricks for them. I have two. The first is to guess which hand is holding a biscuit. I never fail to do this one successfully—I cannot tell why. I suppose it is some rare instinct of mine: whichever hand I choose, right or left, the biscuit is always there.

The other trick is more difficult. My Lady lays a biscuit on the grass, and I am not supposed to touch it until she mentions my name. (My official name, by the way, is Bobbie.) The difficult part about the trick is that she mentions a number of other names first, and I have to wait. For instance, she says: "No, darling, not yet; that's Mother's biscuit!" Or, "That's George's biscuit!" (George is our cat: I shall tell you more about him presently.) And then she mentions some more names, all different, and some of them quite new, until she sees that I can't bear it any longer; and then she cries: "And now it's Bobbie's biscuit!" and I eat it.

Of course, as I say, there are occasional mistakes, but my Lady usually manages to cover them up for me. Once, when I got tired of waiting and gobbled the biscuit when she said it belonged to somebody called Hitler, she explained to the children that it was particularly clever of me to do this, because

Hitler was a person who did not deserve a biscuit at all, and that was why I had done it.

Occasionally other dogs try to join in our games, but I take a pretty firm line with them. If one of them grabs my ball away from me I go straight to my Lady and tell her about it, and she goes and gets it back for me. She seems to be able to do anything she likes with these creatures—always in the sweetest possible way, of course. In fact, I think she is a little too sweet at times, because, when all is said and done, the dogs in Hyde Park are a pretty mixed lot. I know if any of them tries to start a conversation with me I simply turn my back and walk away. My Lady says this shows how well-bred I am: Harry says it is because I am a howling little snob. My Lady must find him somewhat trying at times.

However, we all meet in the evening at dinner—their dinner, that is. My own dinner is served at six o'clock, and as it is the only meal I get in twenty-four hours I make the most of it. Of course I don't count snacks—biscuits in bed, or bits of my Lady's lunch and tea, or buns at the confectioner's, or sandwiches shared with girls behind curtains in shops. These I regard as nothing more than the small courtesies of life, which no gentleman can decline without giving offence. Besides, one must keep up one's strength. And this brings me back to their dinner. I have a basket under the sideboard, and theoretically I stay there all the time. And here is where one has to exercise a good deal of tact. If I come out too soon and trip up somebody carrying plates of soup, Harry is inclined to get what my Lady calls John Bullish about it, and say "Basket!" to me very sternly. My usual procedure then is to crawl back to the basket and lie down, not in it, but beside it, with a deep sigh—just to test the general atmosphere. If this gets a laugh, and it usually does, one can come back and get to work almost immediately; if not, it is a good plan to wait till the next course.

But in the ordinary way I do pretty well at dinner-time. My Lady, bless her, is always good for something; and on special occasions—if I have been to the vet's., or if it has been a wet day, or if I have not eaten the whole of my official dinner—she takes me up on her lap and lets me finish her plate. Then there are occasional guests. These vary a good deal as a class. Some are ridiculously easy, but others have been brought up in a strange school of thought which holds that dogs should never be fed at table. Some of them say so quite rudely; others merely ignore me and make conversation. In these cases I find the best plan is to slip under the table and lay my chin on one of their knees. If I keep it there long enough I nearly always get something, slid furtively under the table-cloth while they keep on talking.

The oddest of them all is Harry himself. Inconsistent, I think is the word. I never met a man so full of good advice. He lectures my Lady incessantly; he is always telling her to wear more clothes, and get more rest, and eat more food instead of giving it to me. Yet he grumbles over the bills for the clothes she does wear, and sits up half the night working himself. As for this food business—why, half the time he is laying down the law to her he is slipping big bits of meat to me under his chair! Yet he keeps on. For instance:

"Angel," he said at dinner only last night, "if you would cover up your beautiful back a bit more and eat what is on your plate instead of giving it to that guzzling tripehound, there might be some chance of your growing up into a nice plump little seraph instead of a secondclass wraith. And don't sit there smiling, as if I wasn't talking seriously! If you aren't good I'll pack you off to Switzerland for another six months—and then you'll be sorry."

"I might not be," replied my Lady. "My Little Boy has never been to Switzerland: he might adore it."

"Your Little Boy would adore any place where free food was available at frequent intervals—but remember this. If he goes to Switzerland you won't be able to bring him back—not without six months' quarantine, anyhow. So it would mean that amount of separation whether you took him with you or left him behind. You'll find it simpler to be good, my girl."

"All right, I'll try," said my Lady, quite meek all of a sudden. "Harry, do you know how long six months is in the life of a dog?"

"Making a rough guess, six months."

"No; that's just it. Three and a half years! Somebody told me the other day that a year of a dog's life is the same as seven years of ours. Do you think I could be separated from my lovely for three and a half years?"

Harry hesitated for a moment before he spoke again. Then he said:

"We shan't be able to keep him for ever, you know, dear. By your own reckoning' when you're forty he'll be well over seventy!"

"I know: that is why I want to make his little life utterly, perfectly happy while it lasts."

She was in one of her rather sad moods to-night: I could see that. So did Harry, and he tried to get her out of it, as he often does, by being funny.

"H'm," he said. "I have a feeling that his little life would last a bit longer if you didn't feed him on boiled salmon, *vol-au vent,* and chocolate ice-cream. That's what he's had to-night, isn't it?"

"Well, you feed him yourself!" My Lady turned to me. "What has your father just given you?" she asked.

"An occasional cutlet bone is a different matter altogether," replied Harry, in what I call his superior voice. Then he laughed.

"We're both humbugs, Kit," he said. "I pamper the little lad, and so do you. I often wonder," he went on presently, "what sort of a job we'd have made of a family. I suppose I'd have spoiled the daughters, while you ruined the sons."

My Lady looked at him rather severely.

"May I ask how many you were proposing that we should have had, darling, if we had had any? A couple of dozen of each?"

"What was your own idea?" asked Harry.

"Just a son. Nothing else."

"Couldn't you have thrown in a daughter—or, say, two? One fair and the other dark: Rosemary, blue eyes, angelic, and rather smug; and Pamela, dark, vivacious, and a bit of a handful. I have often pictured them."

"Have you, dear?"

"Yes. What would you have called your son?"

"Peter."

"I see. Could he have been left-handed, by any chance? There hasn't been a really good left-handed amateur fast bowler for twenty years."

"Yes, darling, of course he could have been left-handed."

"Good!" Harry looked at her with a queer smile, then at me. "As it is," he said, "we've had to come down to this!"

And he gave me another cutlet bone.

FROM MASTER ST. ELMO
BY ST. ELMO
AS TOLD TO CARO SENOUR

The next May we went to a beautiful suburban village, where we now live. I like it the best of all, for I can run all day without a muzzle and every one is kind to me, even if I do run into their houses without an invitation and look all over their dining-room table for their cream-pitchers.

The first thing my mistress did was to take me to the Town Hall and register me a two dollars' worth. She made me tell how old I was, which was six years old last Fourth of July, you remember. I was sent a bright tag stamped No. 1, which meant that I was the first dog registered. You see I am a citizen of the village now, and I have to pay two dollars a year to help support the town, which I am only too proud to be allowed to do. When I was boarding here the year before I was an honorary member of the village, so I did not pay taxes and I appreciate the courtesy bestowed upon me.

When we first came here, we boarded with such a good lady, as we could not get rooms at the hotel, it being filled. This lady took us as a favor and we stayed until our house was ready. She let me sleep on a nice, soft lounge in my master's bed-chamber and gave me good things to eat; so I dearly love her, and when I see her, I jump up and kiss her on the cheek. My family say they cannot understand why I kiss her and no one else, but I will tell them here: it is because she let me go to bed in the evening with her little boy Dexter, and when the big people went up to bed they found us each night asleep together; each one had a pillow, and how I did enjoy this. I'll tell you a cute thing the little boy used to do. When he was sent up in the evening to study his lessons, he would say, "May St. Elmo go up to my room while I study?" and my mistress would say "Yes." So up I would start, but did we study any lessons? Ask this boy friend of mine. We always went to bed tired, so you can guess we had a romp. He was very good to me, and so I am always glad to see him. I was pleased when I found out we were going to have a house to live in, for I like an upstairs to a house since I have learned so well how to climb.

The first day I entered the new house, I was a little disappointed, as I saw nothing but bare floors and walls; but the second day I found to my delight the same old boxes, barrels, pictures, furniture, and rugs, and this time they all looked peaceful and orderly. My mistress was beaming with happiness over the meeting with her old possessions, making a " contrasty " picture to the one of the May before when the hurry-burly impressionistic picture was painted, never to be effaced from my memory, when everything was on the warpath. "Moving-day, May, 1902," is the title of this painting.

Our house is just a little distance from my boy friend's, but I never am allowed to go there alone, as the "Choochoo" car tracks have to be crossed to go there, and the family always hold my collar for fear that I shall be run over. Imagine a big dog like me having to be directed where to go! I do feel so silly, especially when the children, or other dogs are passing. When I had been here a month, I cut my back on a barb-wire fence (such a fence should be condemned), and my mistress thought I had been bitten by a dog; so she hurried me off to the train; but there was no train to Chicago for an hour; then we went to the street-car line, and the conductor said that dogs could not ride on these cars; after a few seconds of pleading, however, I was pushed up some steps into the car. My mistress paid five cents for me, and the man pulled a bell to say that I was paid for; but I had to stay on the back platform, and my mistress stayed with me, for she is very faithful to me. We then got on the elevated train, and I rode in the car, sitting on a seat and looking out of the window. It seemed very funny to be whizzing along in the air, and I wished that Klondyke could have this experience with me. I did not feel quite certain of this flying machine, and when it made me go from side to side, I had the same dizzy feeling that I had when I took my first ride on that IRON HORSE. My! but I have learned lots since the first day that I left Kansas, and I do wish that all the dogs of that windy place could learn as much. I have a tender spot in my heart for Kansas, for it was bright and sunny there even if the wind did blow all my hair off.

Well, I got into Chicago and down to the veterinary surgeon who examined me one dollar and a half's worth, and said it was no bite, only a cut by wire. I knew how I got it, but my stupid mistress could not understand me. She was greatly rejoiced, and telephoned my master to come and meet us and take us back to the country. I forgot to tell you that I had two severe operations at different times, and two tumors removed from my knee by this splendid surgeon, Doctor White, and he said that I was a hero, for I stayed on the operating-table, and they did not have to tie my mouth. I watched his performance and tried to think it did not hurt, as I felt sure he was doing it for my good, so I was patient. Let me tell you how I got those horrid bumps. In our Calumet house was a window bench just wide enough for me to lie on, and such a splendid place to see all that was going on out-side, and still be on the inside away from the flies (when I say flies I shake all over). The family had it nicely padded when I came to live with them, but after my constant camping on it, the cushion wore thin, so that every time I jumped down I scraped my knees and soon made a lump; then again, I had to wear a harness when I was going on a trip, and when I would lie down the buckle came where my knee did, so that also helped to enlarge this bump. My family did not know this or I never should have suffered, for as soon as they found out what caused my troubles, they had a new window cushion for me and the hard buckle changed, but not until I had cost them a "twenty-dollar william" for operations. My harness was made where they made harnesses for horses, and it was all right at first, but I grew so fast that the buckle could not keep up with me, so we became a misfit.

There are some very nice and polite dogs out here. My very particular friend is "Captain," a brown setter. We understand each other and have great sport. My nearest neighbor is a brown water-spaniel, "Brownie," but he is a little particular about getting acquainted too soon; so we just speak. I think he is a wee bit jealous, as he has a young master and mistress who are very dear to him, and he does not want any one else to share their petting; then too, he was here first, and " possession is nine points in the law, " so I have only one point. Well, we do not quarrel, and as my family and "Brownie's" family agree, of course we shall some day be friends. I shall, however, ask him to my next birthday party, but I hope he will not bring me a woolly-puzzle dog. "Buster Brown" gave me a pointer on how to have parties, so I am going to try it next time, only I hope my presents will not be returned. I shall be "foxy" and tell my friends to bring me things to eat; so that they can be consumed before the time to return them comes. Let me think! I should like best of all a bone, for that is what I never get, as my family say that bones make me ill, and the doctor also said I could not have them as my digestive machinery inside was too delicate to grind up bones; next would come English walnuts, next cake, then candy, then ice-cream—I could eat about a quart of that, sure. Oh yes! I forgot vaseline! I am very partial to that; it's next to butter, which I think comes second in my likes. I have a good many toys. This Christmas I received in my stockings a rubber humpty-dumpty doll, a squeaky ball, a bean bag from Aunt Lillie, a new blue ribbon, and a bath. I seem to get baths on all holidays, so that didn't count as a present. When I first came out here I could not find my playthings because the family was so slow in unpacking my things; they thought mine the least important, but I considered them first; so I had to play with sticks until one day I saw some nice little children playing near our house. One of the children had something in her hand, and as I was very curious to see what it was (for at a distance it looked very much like my old woolly-dog, after the battle), I walked up to the wee girl and took it out of her hand and ran home as fast as I could. My! how she did yell; that was a funny thing for her to do, don't you think? When I got home, it was a poor, forlorn pussy-cat looking very much like my ungrateful puzzle-dog. She had no eyes, and only one ear, which made you think she was lopsided; her nose and mouth had united, but she had a tail, the same kind of tail that my poor doggie had. I was very careful about the workmanship of her interior, so I handled her quite carefully. My mistress tried to find the owner of pussy, but she could not, so she left her in plain sight on the walk for some days; but would you believe that nobody would own her? At last I took pity on her and brought her into the house and she is now on my mistress's desk as she is writing at my dictation to-day. I love her best of all my playthings, for I always did love the poor homeless animals the best.

FROM HIS APOLOGIES
AS TOLD TO RUDYARD KIPLING

Master, this is Thy Servant.
    He is rising eight weeks old.
He is mainly Head and Tummy.
    His legs are uncontrolled.
But Thou hast forgiven his ugliness,
    and settled him on Thy knee...
Art Thou content with Thy Servant?
    He is *very* comfy with Thee.

Master, behold a Sinner!
    He hath done grievous wrong.
He hath defiled Thy Premises
    through being kept in too long.
Wherefore his nose has been rubbed in the dirt,
    and his self-respect has been bruiséd.
Master, pardon Thy Sinner,
    and see he is properly looséd.

Master—again Thy Sinner!
　　This that was once Thy Shoe,
He hath found and taken and carried aside,
　　as fitting matter to chew.
Now there is neither blacking nor tongue,
　　and the Housemaid has us in tow.
Master, remember Thy Servant is young,
　　and tell her to let him go!

Master, extol Thy Servant!
　　He hath met a most Worthy Foe!
There has been fighting all over the Shop—
　　and into the Shop also!
Till cruel umbrellas parted the strife
　　(or I might have been choking him yet).
But Thy Servant has had the Time of his Life
　　—and now shall we call on the vet?

Master, behold Thy Servant!
　　Strange children came to play,
And because they fought to caress him,
　　Thy Servant wentedst away.
But now that the Little Beasts have gone,
　　he has returned to see

(Brushed—with his Sunday collar on—)
    what they left over from tea.

Master, pity Thy Servant!
    He is deaf and three parts blind,
He cannot catch Thy Commandments.
    He cannot read Thy Mind.
Oh, leave him not in his loneliness;
    nor make him that kitten's scorn.
He has had none other God than thee
    since the year that he was born,

Lord, look down on Thy Servant!
    Bad things have come to pass,
There is no heat in the midday sun
    nor health in the wayside grass.
His bones are full of an old disease—
    his torments run and increase.
Lord, make haste with Thy Lightnings
    and grant him a quick release!

FROM CAT AND DOG
BY CAPTAIN
AS TOLD TO JULIA C. MAITLAND

I am going to relate the history of a pleasant and prosperous life; for though a few misfortunes may have befallen me, my pleasures have far exceeded them, and especially I have been treated with such constant cordiality and kindness as would not fail to insure the happiness of man or beast. But though I have no reason to complain of my destiny, it is a remarkable fact, that my principal happiness has been produced by conforming myself to unfavorable circumstances, and reconciling myself to an unnatural fate.

Nature herself did well by me. I am a fine setter, of a size that a Newfoundland dog could not despise, and a beauty that a Blenheim spaniel might envy. With a white and brown curly coat, drooping ears, bushy tail, a delicate pink nose, and good-natured brown eyes, active, strong, honest, gentle, and obedient, I have always felt a conscious pride and pleasure in being a thoroughly well-bred dog.

My condition in life was peculiarly comfortable. I was brought up in an old manor-house inhabited by a gentleman and his daughter, with several respectable and good-natured servants. My education was conducted with care, and from my earliest youth I had the advantage of an introduction into good society. I was not, indeed, allowed to come much into the drawing-room as my master said I was too large for a drawing-room dog; but I had the range of the lower part of the house, and constant admittance to his study, where I was welcome to share his fireside while he read the newspapers or received visitors. I took great interest in his friends; and by means of listening to their conversation watching them from under my eyelids while they thought I was asleep, and smelling them carefully, I could form a sufficiently just estimate of their characters to regulate my own conduct towards them. Though a polite dog both by birth and breeding, I was too honest and independent to show the same respect and cordiality towards those whom I like and those whom I despised; and though very grateful for the smallest favors from persons I esteemed, no flattery, caresses, or benefactions could induce me to strike up an intimacy with one who did not please me. If I had been able to speak, I should have expressed my opinions without ceremony; and it often surprised me that my master, who could say what he pleased, did not quarrel with people and tell them all their faults openly. I thought, if I had been he, I would have had many a fight with intruders, to whom he was not only civil himself, but compelled me to be so too. I have often observed that it appears proper for human beings to observe a kind of respect even towards persons they dislike; a line of conduct which *brutes* cannot understand.

However, I was not without my own methods of showing my sentiments. If I felt indifferent or contemptuous towards a person entering the room, I merely opened one eye and yawned at him. If he attempted any compliments, calling me "Good Captain," "Fine Dog," and trying to pat me, I shook off his hand, and rising from my rug, turned once around, and curling my tail under me, sank down again to my repose without taking any further notice of him. But occasionally my master admitted visitors whom I considered as such highly improper acquaintances for him, that I could scarcely restrain my indignation. I knew I must note bite them, though, in my own opinion, it would have been by far the best thing to do; I did not dare so much as to bark at them, for my master objected even to that expression of feeling:

but I could not resist receiving them with low growls; during their visit I never took my eyes off them for a moment, and I made a point of following them to the door, and seeing them safe off the premises. Others, on the contrary, I regarded with the highest confidence and esteem. Their visits gave almost as much pleasure to me as my master, and I took pains to show my friendship by every means in my power; leaving the fireside to meet them, wagging my tail, shaking a paw with them the moment I was asked, and sitting with my nose resting on their lap.

But I took no unwelcome liberties; for I was gifted with a particular power of discriminating between those who really liked me, and those who only tolerated me out of politeness. Upon the latter I never willingly intruded, though I have been sometimes obliged to submit to a hypocritical pat bestowed on me for the sake of my young mistress; but a real friend of dogs I recognized at a glance, whether lady or gentleman, so that I could safely place my paw in the whitest hand, or rest my head against the gayest dress, without fear of a repulse.

The person I loved best in the world was my master; or rather, I should say, he was the person for whom I had the highest respect. My love was bestowed in at least an equal degree upon my young mistress, his daughter Lily, in whose every action I took a deep interest.

She was a graceful, gentle little creature, whom I could have knocked down and trampled upon in a minute; but though my strength was so superior to hers there was no one whom I was so ready to obey. A word or look from Lily managed me completely; and her gentle warning of "Oh, Captain," has often recalled me to good manners when I was on the point of breaking out into fury against some obnoxious person. Willing subject as I was, I yet looked upon myself in some manner as her guardian and protector, and it would have fared ill with man or beast who had attempted to molest her.

As I mentioned before, I was not allowed to come much into the drawing-room; but Lily found many opportunities of noticing me. I always sat at the foot of the stairs to watch for her as she came down to the breakfast-room, when she used to pat my head and say, "How do you do, good Captain? Nice dog," as she passed. Then I wagged my tail, and was very happy. I think I should have moped half the day if I had missed Lily's morning greeting. After breakfast she came into the garden, and brought me pieces of toast, and gave me lessons in what she considered clever ways of eating. I should have preferred snapping at her gifts and bolting them down my own throat in my own way; but, to please Lily, I learned to sit patiently watching the most tempting buttered crust on the ground under my nose, when she said, "Trust, Captain!" never dreaming of touching it till she gave the word of command, "Now it is paid for;" when I ate it in a genteel and deliberate manner. Having achieved such a conquest over myself, I thought my education was complete; but Lily had further *refinements* in store. She made me hold the piece of toast on my very nose while she counted *ten,* and at the word *ten* I was to toss it up in the air, and catch it in my mouth as it came down. I was a good while learning this trick, for I did not at all see the use of it. I could smell the bread distinctly as it lay on my nose, and why I should not eat it at once I never could understand. I have often peeped in at the dining-room window to see if my master and mistress ate their food in the same manner; but though I have sometimes seen them perform my first feat of sitting quietly before their plates, I never once saw them put their meat on their noses and catch it. However, it was Lily's pleasure, and that was enough for me.

She also taught me to shut the door at her command. This was rather a noisy performance, as I could only succeed by running against the door with my whole weight; but it gave Lily so much satisfaction, that she used to open the door a dozen times a day, on purpose for me to bang it.

Another favorite amusement of hers was making me look at myself in the glass. I grew used to this before long; but the first time that she set a mirror before me on the ground, I confess that I was a good deal astonished and puzzled. At the first glance I took the dog in the glass for an enemy and rival intruding upon my dominions, so I naturally prepared for a furious attack upon him. He appeared equally ready, and I perceived that he was quite my match. But when after a great deal of barking and violence, nobody was hurt, I fancied that the looking-glass was the barrier which prevented our coming to close quarters, and that my adversary had intrenched himself behind it in the most cowardly manner. Determined that he should not profit by his baseness, I cleverly walked round behind the glass, intending to seize him and give him a thorough shaking; but there I found nothing! I dashed to the front once more; there he stood as fierce as ever. Again behind his battlements—nobody! till after repeated trials, I began to have a glimmering of the state of the case; and feeling rather ashamed of having been so taken in, I declined further contest, and lay down quietly before the mirror to contemplate my own image, and reflect upon my own reflection.

A DOG'S EYE VIEW
AS TOLD TO AMELIA JOSEPHINE BURR

The people whom I take to walk
    I love and yet deplore,
Such things of real importance
    They persistently ignore.
The sights and smells that thrill me
    They stolidly pass by,
Then stop and stare in rapture
    At nothing in the sky.

They waste such time in stopping
    To look at things like flowers.
They pick the dullest places
    To settle down for hours.
Sometimes I really wonder
    If they can hear and smell;
Such vital things escape them—
    And yet they mean so well!

FROM A THOROUGHBRED MONGREL

AS TOLD TO STEPHEN TOWNSEND

I felt sorry for Jock. I always go down into the country for a little ratting and rabbiting in the summer, and this having been an unusually heavy season in town, my people have rented his people's kennel for six months. Jock had allowed his family to run over to the Continent alone, Jock not being fond of railway travelling, and he found himself in the anomalous position of being a stranger on his own premises. But there was no good growling about it. Besides, it was probably his own fault. *My* people would no more think of travelling without me than they would of chasing a hare across a field. If they had any such scheme, I should put my hind-paw down on it promptly. I should appeal to their reason. I should—SIT UP. I never knew that to fail even with the most scentless and incanine of Humans. When a dog has any trouble with a well-bred Biped one may bet one's last biscuit it is generally his own fault. Of course, there is such a thing as being *too* kind—even to Human Beings—and then they are apt to presume. For instance, in town I should never dream of going out for a walk without proper attendance. In the country I often go rabbiting alone (Humans are so slow in their movements and so apt to get lost), but I never tell my people lest they should take advantage of it and shirk their proper responsibilities. I have known some really good Bipeds ruined in this way. They get careless and inattentive, and one has always to be reminding them of their duties. They have the same trouble with the lower breeds amongst themselves, bad servants, careless tradespeople, and others. The more consideration you show such animals, the more they abuse it. The point is to nip these things in the *kitten* and not wait to fight them as cats. The other day one of my people wanted me to fetch my own collar. I felt this might prove a dangerous precedent, so I sacrificed my reputation for intelligence to my principles, and, smiling in an imbecile manner, pretended not to understand. With Humans, if you want a thing done, never do it yourself. However, it was difficult to drive anything into Jock's thick head. He wasn't a bit intellectual, and thought more of chasing a sheep on the hillside than of psychological discussion.

"Look here, Jock," I said, rolling lazily over on to my back and stretching my paws stiffly in the air as an indication to my master that he might come and rub my tummer, "growl as you will, you can't deny that Human Beings are not only useful but intelligent—highly intelligent—animals."

"In what way?" snapped Jock, in a voice that might be heard in the adjoining county.

"In many ways," I replied with studied mildness, and assuming a more dignified position; "but first let me tell you that in the best circles it is not the custom to converse in barks suggestive of a bull, or of that most detestable of Human inventions, the horn of a motor-car. You are not addressing a flock of sheep, but an educated lady, who allows no dog, big or little, to speak to her like that. And I'll, further, trouble you for my tail when you've done lying on it."

Jock apologised, and, to conceal his discomfiture, snapped at a fly, which he missed. It is often the way with these big country collies. They have no manners and less education. Had it not been for my desire to improve Jock, I should have left him to himself and his sheep-dreams. Personally, I had had unusual educational advantages. As a puppy I was brought up in the house of a famous scientist, and had the free run of the library. I simply *devoured* literature. I should have remained scientific to this day, and Jock would never have experienced the advantage of knowing me, had I not made a horrible discovery. The scientist proved to be a criminal of the worst type. Amongst his books I found what was simply a treatise on murder under the title "Experiments on Living Animals." I read—and destroyed it. A difference of opinion followed, and I felt I must dispose of him. The next time I took him a walk, I allowed him to get lost.

I had seen more of the world in a week than Jock had seen in a lifetime, and it seemed my duty, as an educated Skye, to enlighten his bucolic mind.

"Yes, Jock," I continued, "Human Beings are useful and intelligent in many ways. They are amusing to caress, clean in their habits, comfortable to sit on. They never tire of making things for us to destroy, they—"

"See here," broke in Jock, laying his head on his front paws and looking me straight in the face; "when I was young and went in for sheep, I kept a shepherd for the show of the thing. I might as well have kept a scarecrow. He could no more have brought a flock of sheep down the hillside without me than he could have caught a hare in the open field. Who was the more useful and intelligent, he or I?"

"But, my dear Jock—"

"I have a friend down in the village," continued Jock, not allowing me to get a bark in edgeways, "an eccentric old dog called 'Fido' who keeps a blind man. Fido found him groping about in the lanes one day as helpless as a new-born pup, took him home, and made a pet of him—I'd as soon make a pet of a dead sheep. Fido is tied to him for the rest of his life, has to take him out every morning, drag him about by a string, carry a tin can around and collect biscuits for him, take him back to kennel and watch him through the night, and yet you call Human Beings useful and intelligent."

"My dear Jock, you mustn't take shepherds and blind men as representative breeds of Humans. Some of us, out of philanthropy (and there are no philanthropists like ourselves) keep a blind man; some of you collies have a taste for shepherds, but they are both confessedly mongrels, being the only Bipeds who are *allowed* to live with us without being expected to pay a licence."

"Yes, but they are not the only Bipeds who do."

"What do you mean?"

"I mean," said Jock, scratching his ear with his hind-paw in a knowing manner, "that Humans are often *frauds,* and what dog would condescend to be that?"

I turned one eye on Jock's bone, and one eye on Jock, cocked my left ear, and said nothing.

"Yes, frauds," repeated Jock, lumbering up on to his great feet and giving himself a huge shake to cover his confusion. "I know a spaniel, a regular aristocrat and very proud of his descent, who took up with a medical man, a real Vet., mind you, not one of the so-called doctors who attend to Humans only—a man who ought to have had some sense of the respect due to a dog. Now what do you think? The man actually was *unlicensed.* Of course they fined him heavily. But imagine the humiliation of my friend, who had to appear in court! I'd like to *worry* a man like that."

"Which sentiment, Jock, is a disgrace to caninity. You make me feel that the more I see of dogs, such dogs as you, the more I like Humans."

"I'll be *muzzled* if I do," said Jock, scratching himself violently.

"Don't swear, Jock," I replied quietly, "and as you've no manners you'll excuse me leaving you. The gong has just sounded and I see my master looking for me."

"Looking for you," growled Jock savagely; "what does he want to *look* for? Why can't he scent you? What's the good of Humans? They can't run as fast as we can, they can't see better, they can't hear as well, and as for scent, they could hardly point a sewer at twenty paces."

To these rude remarks I did not condescend to reply, but, following my master into the house, sought my customary place under the table.

NINETY-TWO

LONE DOG
AS TOLD TO IRENE R. MCLEOD

I'm a lean dog, a keen dog, a wild dog and lone;
I'm a rough dog, a tough dog, a howling on my own;
I'm a bad dog, a mad dog, teasing silly sheep;
I love to sit and howl by the moon, to keep fat souls from sleep.

I'll never be a lap dog, licking dirty feet,
A sleek dog, a meek dog, cringing for my meat.
Not for me the fireside, the well filled plate,
But shut door, and sharp stone, and cuff, and kick, and hate.

Not for me the other dogs, running by my side,
Some have run a short while but none of them would bide.
O mine is still the lone trail, the hard trail, the best,
Wide wind, and wild stars, and the hunger of the quest!

NOTICE GIVEN
AS TOLD TO BERTON BRALEY

I'm in disgrace
  And degradation
And yet I *told* Them
  The situation;
I whined a lot
  And walked the floor
And went and sat
  By the outer door.

But They weren't paying
  The least attention,
They didn't hear
  When I tried to mention,

They wouldn't listen
  To my sad yelp
—So then what happened
  I couldn't help!

I gave Them hints
  And if they scorn them
They cannot say
  That I didn't warn Them!

FROM THE RUBAIYAT OF OMAR KI-YI
AS TOLD TO BURGES JOHNSON

VIII

Let's hunt for cats, and in the fire of spring
Our winter garment of repentance fling.
   The leash of time has such a little reach,
And stops us short ere we have had our fling.

IX

Will puppyhood ne'er leave me? Still I wail
For morsels from some tightly covered pail,—
   Or bay the moon; and was it yesterday
I caught myself pursuing my own tail?

X

Myself when young much eager leisure spent
Watching a rabbit-hole with grim intent,
   And never knew, through all those patient hours
He had another door where out he went.

FROM TOLD BY DIGGER

AS TOLD TO JOHN DAVIS

Digger describes himself as "a professional dog from Austrailia, my line of business being sheep." He has come to London with his master and, having gotten lost, has been adopted by an Aberdeen terrier, Scotty, who is showing him around...

We went to Soho one day. When I say we went to Soho, I mean we were drawn there by the nice smells; there were smells other than nice, too—unless one happens to be fond of garlic, which I am not. We felt rather like foreigners in this part, owing to a difficulty in understanding the various brands of language spoken by most of the people.

We met a dog—a strange breed to us—who asked a question in some funny tongue. We could do nothing but blankly stare at him; as he departed he called us "Gracias," and Scotty wanted to fasten to him on the chance of this being an insult, but discretion *and* the presence of a number of lingo-speaking dogs persuaded us to retain a dignified silence. One particularly appetising smell led us to a place where dinner was being served. We strolled inside looking expectant and—came out again hurriedly. We were not welcome, judging by the number of things thrown and the nasty remarks spat at us by an unmannerly cat. Scotty said that that cat was "no lady"—I suppose not, because I had heard somebody call it "Peter." We had a yarn with one dog—a Cockney this time—who told us that his boss always spoke to him in Cockney, but preferred for the sake of the business to use broken French in addressing his customers; this dog's speciality was policemen, and he held down a permanent job in a night club, what-ever that may mean. I liked the look of a monkey we came across. Scotty didn't and said so; the monkey retaliated by seizing him by the short hairs, and Scotty was sorry he had spoken. He cheered up considerably, however, when we left Soho, and was positively elated when we came across a kilted piper playing in the streets. One could almost imagine that Scotty was swinging a "sporran" in the manner of his countrymen by the look of his chest as he waddled along. I was not so impressed, and said that I should like to be about when the man "let the cat out of the bag," which remark Scotty said was not funny.

A peculiar squeaking sound attracted us into a side street, where we found a circle of small people—and some large ones—watching a Punch and Judy show; we, of course, were most interested in the Toby dog, who seemed embarrassed by the prolonged applause we tendered him.

"I wish you dogs would lose yourselves," he said from the stage, "you make me forget my part!"

"That's the worst of you theatrical people," barked Scotty as we left the stalls, "you're too confoundedly temperamental."

We did a little "bus-hopping" after this; there was only one thing which prevented us from having some perfectly good free rides—and that was the conductor's boot! A woman selling flowers was very rude to us when we sniffed around her basket; the remarks were most uncalled for—we were not going to eat her old flowers! Some pictures drawn on the footpath suffered badly as we rushed around a corner; we had scampered across them before we realized that they were there. Scotty supposed that in consequence there would be more letters to the papers about dogs not appreciating art.

We struck up an acquaintanceship with a dog in Fleet Street

who runs a very interesting little business; everyone seems to know him—he makes a tidy income by stopping people and demanding pennies! Scotty was pop-eyed with admiration, and in course of conversation asked where the pennies were hidden; our friend wasn't giving *that* information away to an Aberdeen terrier! No wonder the boss said Fleet Street is hard—even the dogs are hard-boiled there!

Continuing up the "street," we came to a very large building with a very large round roof—St. Paul's, I think it is called. Here we saw *millions* of pigeons with nothing to do except be fed by people who apparently had nothing to do except feed them. I am quite sure, however, that if dogs were fed in the same manner they would not be nearly so nicely behaved. One pigeon alighted on Scotty's back; I think that he was inclined to resent the familiarity. "Flighty, I call that bird," he said; "but still, one can't say much to a pigeon."

Further walking took us through streets where most men wore shiny tall hats and carried little bags; I wondered—like humans, we dogs think a lot about food—whether that was how they carried lunch! Scotty's instincts give him a great respect for the City; I must confess I found it a little dull.

On the way homeward I told Scotty that my boss had broken out in a fresh place. He had gone out in the morning carrying a lot of funny sticks in a bag and wearing the weirdest clothes I have yet seen on him—Plus Fours he called them—they looked like bags to me. My Scotch friend could see nothing funny in this and was inclined to reprove me for facetiousness in regard to a sacred subject. "He was only going to play gawf, you fool!" he said.

Scotty seems to have a new respect for my boss.

pete s theology
BY PETE THE PUP
AS TOLD TO DON MARQUIS

god made seas to play beside
and rugs to cover dogs
god made cars for holidays
and beetles under logs

god made kitchens so thered be
dinners to eat and scraps
god made beds so pups could crawl
under them for naps

god made license numbers so theyd find
lost pups and bring them home
god made garbage buckets too
to pry in when you roam

god made tennis shoes to chew
and here and there a hat
but i cant see why god should make
mehitabel the cat.

THE BLOODHOUND SPEAKS
AS TOLD TO A.C. GATE

I am the dog world's best detective.
My sleuthing nose is so effective
I sniff the guilty at a distance
And then they lead a doomed exstence.
My well-known record for convictions
Has earned me lots of maledictions
From those whose trail of crime I scented
And sent to prison, unlamented.
Folks either must avoid temptation
Or face my nasal accusation.

THE REAL REASON
AS TOLD TO JOE WALKER

They call me "clever," but I get so tired
Of being praised and sloppily admired
For doing silly things—I "die," I beg,
I growl, when told, or "shake" a friendly leg;
Such foolish stunts I do with utmost ease,
One feels an idiot, but it seems to please,
And, after all, it would be a mistake
To sneer at sugar or to turn down cake.
Still, I *am* "clever," though folks do not know
Why I agree with them that this is so,
But here's the reason—*every blessed day*
I please myself and get my own sweet way.

THE MIXER II
BY FIDO
AS TOLD TO P.G. WODEHOUSE

It was one of those things which are really nobody's fault. It was not the chauffeur's fault, and it was not mine. I was having a friendly turn-up with a pal of mine on the side-walk; he ran across the road; I ran after him; and the car came round the corner and hit me. It must have been going pretty slow, or I should have been killed. As it was, I just had the breath knocked out of me. You know how you feel when the butcher catches you just as you are edging out of the shop with a bit of meat. It was like that.

I wasn't taking much interest in things for awhile but when I did I found that I was the centre of a group of three—the chauffeur, a small boy, and the small boy's nurse.

The small boy was very well-dressed, and looked delicate. He was crying.

"Poor doggie," he said, "poor doggie."

"It wasn't my fault, Master Peter," said the chauffeur respectfully. "He run out into the road before I seen him."

"That's right," I put in, for I didn't want to get the man into trouble.

"Oh, he's not dead," said the small boy. "He barked."

"He growled," said the nurse. "Come away, Master Peter. He might bite you."

Women are trying sometimes. It is almost as if they deliberately misunderstood.

"I won't come away. I'm going to take him home with me and send for the doctor to come and see him. He's going to be my dog."

This sounded all right. Goodness knows I am no snob, and

can rough it when required, but I do like comfort when it comes my way, and it seemed to me that this was where I got it. And I liked the boy. He was the right sort.

The nurse, a very unpleasant woman, had to make objections.

"Master Peter! You can't take him home, a great, rough, fierce, common dog! What would your mother say?"

"I'm going to take him home," repeated the child, with a determination which I heartily admired, "and he's going to be my dog. I shall call him Fido."

There's always a catch in these good things. Fido is a name I particularly detest. All dogs do. There was a dog called that that I knew once, and he used to get awfully sick when we shouted it out after him in the street. No doubt there have been respectable dogs called Fido, but to my mind it is a name like Aubrey or Clarence. You may be able to live it down, but you start handicapped. However, one must take the rough with the smooth, and I was prepared to yield the point.

"If you wait, Master Peter, your father will buy you a beautiful, lovely dog..."

"I don't want a beautiful, lovely dog. I want this dog."

The slur did not wound me. I have no illusions about my looks. Mine is an honest, but not a beautiful, face.

"It's no use talking," said the chauffeur, grinning. "He means to have him. Shove him in, and let's be getting back, or they'll be thinking His Nibs has been kidnapped."

So I was carried to the car. I could have walked, but I had an idea that I had better not. I had made my hit as a crippled dog, and a crippled dog I intended to remain till things got more settled down.

The chauffeur started the car off again. What with the shock I had had and the luxury of riding in a motor-car, I was a little distrait, and I could not say how far we went. But it must have been miles and miles, for it seemed a long time afterwards that we stopped at the biggest house I have ever seen. There were smooth lawns and flower-beds, and men in overalls, and fountains and trees, and, away to the right, kennels with about a million dogs in them, all pushing their noses through the bars and shouting. They all wanted to know who I was and what prizes I had won, and then I realized that I was moving in high society.

I let the small boy pick me up and carry me into the house, though it was all he could do, poor kid, for I was some weight. He staggered up the steps and along a great hall, and then let me flop on the carpet of the most beautiful room you ever saw. The carpet was a yard thick.

There was a woman sitting in a chair, and as soon as she saw me she gave a shriek.

"I told Master Peter you would not be pleased, m'lady," said the nurse, who seemed to have taken a positive dislike to me, "but he would bring the nasty brute home."

"He's not a nasty brute, mother. He's my dog, and his name's Fido. John ran over him in the car, and I brought him home to live with us. I love him."

This seemed to make an impression. Peter's mother looked as if she were weakening.

"But, Peter, dear, I don't know what your father will say. He's so particular about dogs. All his dogs are prize-winners, pedigree dogs. This is such a mongrel."

"A nasty, rough, ugly, common dog, m'lady," said the nurse, sticking her oar in in an absolutely uncalled for way.

Just then a man came into the room.

"What on earth?" he said, catching sight of me.

"It's a dog Peter has brought home. He says he wants to

keep him."

"I'm *going* to keep him," corrected Peter firmly.

I do like a child that knows his own mind. I was getting fonder of Peter every minute. I reached up and licked his hand.

"See! He knows he's my dog, don't you, Fido? He licked me."

"But, Peter, he looks so fierce." This unfortunately, is true. I do look fierce. It is rather a misfortune for a perfectly peaceful dog. "I'm sure it's not safe your having him."

"He's my dog, and his name's Fido. I am going to tell cook to give him a bone."

His mother looked at his father, who gave rather a nasty laugh.

"My dear Helen," he said, "ever since Peter was born, ten years ago, he has not asked for a single thing, to the best of my recollection, which he has not got. Let us be consistent. I don't approve of this caricature of a dog, but if Peter wants him, I suppose he must have him."

"Very well. But the first sign of viciousness he shows, he shall be shot. He makes me nervous."

So they left it at that, and I went off with Peter to get my bone.

After lunch, he took me to the kennels to introduce me to the other dogs. I had to go, but I knew it would not be pleasant, and it wasn't. Any dog will tell you what these prize-ribbon dogs are like. Their heads are so swelled they have to go into their kennels backwards.

It was just as I had expected. There were mastiffs, terriers, poodles, spaniels, bulldogs, sheepdogs, and every other kind of dog you can imagine, all prize-winners at a hundred shows, and every single dog in the place just shoved his head back and laughed himself sick. I never felt so small in my life, and I was glad when it was over and Peter took me off to the stables.

I was just feeling that I never wanted to see another dog in my life, when a terrier ran out, shouting. As soon as he saw me, he came up inquiringly, walking very stiff-legged, as terriers do when they see a stranger.

"Well," he said, "and what particular sort of a prize-winner are you? Tell me all about the ribbons they gave you at the Crystal Palace, and let's get it over."

He laughed in a way that did me good.

"Guess again!" he said. "Did you take me for one of the nuts in the kennels? My name's Jack, and I belong to one of the grooms."

"What!" I cried. "You aren't Champion Bowlegs Royal or anything of that sort! I'm glad to meet you."

So we rubbed noses as friendly as you please. It was a treat meeting one of one's own sort. I had had enough of those high-toned dogs who look at you as if you were something the garbage-man had forgotten to take away.

"He would take me," I said, pointing to Peter.

"Oh, you're his latest, are you? Then you're all right—while it lasts."

"How do you mean, while it lasts?"

"Well, I'll tell you what happened to me. Young Peter took a great fancy to me once. Couldn't do enough for me for awhile. Then he got tired of me, and out I went. You see, the trouble is that while he's a perfectly good kid, he has always had everthing he wanted since he was born, and he gets tired of things pretty easy. It was a toy railway that finished me. Directly he got that, I might not have been on the earth. It was lucky for me that Dick, my present old man, happened to want a dog to keep down the rats, or goodness knows what might not have happened to me. They aren't keen on dogs here unless they've pulled down enough blue ribbons to sink a ship, and mongrels like you and me—no offence—don't last long. I expect you noticed that the grown-ups didn't exactly cheer when you arrived?"

"They weren't chummy."

"Well, take it from me, your only chance is make them chummy. If you do something to please them, they might let you stay on, even though Peter was tired of you."

"What sort of thing?"

"That's for you to think out. I couldn't find one. I might tell you to save Peter from drowning. You don't need a pedigree to do that. But you can't drag the kid to the lake and push him in. That's the trouble. A dog gets so few opportunities. But, take it from me, if you don't do something within two weeks to make yourself solid with the adults, you can make your will. In two weeks Peter will have forgotten all about you. It's not his fault. It's the way he has been brought up. His father has all the money on earth, and Peter's the only child. You can't blame him. All I say is look out for yourself. Well, I'm glad to have met you. Drop in again when you can. I can give you some good ratting, and I have a bone or two put away. So long."

It worried me badly what Jack had said. I couldn't get it out of my mind. If it hadn't been for that, I should have had a great time, for Peter certainly made a lot of fuss of me. He treated me as if I were the only friend he had.

And, in a way, I was. When you are the only son of a man who has all the money in the world, it seems that you aren't allowed to be like an ordinary kid. They coop you up, as if you were something precious that would be contaminated by contact with other children. In all the time that I was at the house I never met another child. Peter had everything in the world, except someone of his own age to go round with; and that made him different from any of the kids I had known.

He liked talking to me. I was the only person round who really understood him. He would talk by the hour and I would listen with my tongue hanging out and nod now and then.

It was worth listening to, what he used to tell me. He told me the most surprising things. I didn't know, for instance, that there were any Red Indians in England but he said there was a chief named Big Cloud who lived in the rhododendron bushes by the lake. I never found him, though I went carefully through them one day. He also said that there were pirates on the island in the lake. I never saw them either.

What he liked telling me about best was the city of gold and precious stones which you came to if you walked far enough through the woods at the back of the stables. He was always meaning to go off there some day, and, from the way he described it, I didn't blame him. It was certainly a pretty good city. It was just right for dogs, too, he said, having bones and liver and sweet cakes there and everything else a dog could want. It used to make my mouth water to listen to him.

We were never apart. I was with him all day, and I slept on the mat in his room at night. But all the time I couldn't get out of my mind what Jack had said. I nearly did once, for it seemed to me that I was so necessary to Peter that nothing could separate us; but just as I was feeling safe his father gave him a toy aeroplane, which flew when you wound it up. The day he got it, I might not have been on the earth. I trailed along, but he hadn't a word to say to me.

Well, something went wrong with the aeroplane the second day, and it wouldn't fly, and then I was in solid again, but I had done some hard thinking and I knew just where I stood. I was the newest toy, that's what I was, and something newer might come along at any moment, and then it would be the finish for me. The only thing for me was to do something to impress the adults, just as Jack had said.

Goodness knows I tried. But everything I did turned out wrong. There seemed to be a fate about it. One morning, for example, I was trotting round the house early and I met a fellow I could have sworn was a burglar. He wasn't one of the family, and he wasn't one of the servants, and he was hanging round the house in a most suspicious way. I chased him up a tree, and it wasn't till the family came down to breakfast, two hours later, that I found that he was a guest who had arrived overnight, and had come out early to enjoy the freshness of the morning and the sun shining on the lake, he being that sort of man. That didn't help me much.

Next, I got in wrong with the boss, Peter's father. I don't know why. I met him out in the park with another man, both carrying bundles of sticks and looking very serious and earnest. Just as I reached him, the boss lifted one of the sticks and hit a small white ball with it. He had never seemed to want to play with me before, and I took it as a great compliment I raced after the ball, which he had hit quite a long way, picked it up in my mouth, and brought it back to him. I laid it at his feet, and smiled up at him.

"Hit it again," I said.

He wasn't pleased at all. He said all sorts of things and tried to kick me, and that night, when he thought I was not listening, I heard him telling his wife that I was a pest and would have to be got rid of. That made me think.

And then I put the lid on it. With the best intentions in the world I got myself into such a mess that I thought the end had come.

It happened one afternoon in the drawing-room. There were visitors that day—women, and women seem fatal to me. I was in the background, trying not to be seen, for, though I had been brought in by Peter the family never liked my coming into the drawing-room. I was hoping for a piece of cake and not paying much attention to the conversation, which was all about somebody called Toto, whom I had not met. Peter's mother said Toto was a sweet little darling, he was; and one of the visitors said Toto had not been at all himself that day and she was quite worried. And a good lot more about how all that Toto would ever take for dinner was a little white meat of chicken, chopped up fine. It was not very interesting, and I had allowed my attention to wander.

And just then, peeping round the corner of my chair to see if there were any signs of cake, what should I see but a great beastly brute of a rat. It was standing right beside the visitor, drinking milk out of a saucer, if you please!

I may have my faults, but procrastination in the presence of rats is not one of them. I didn't hesitate for a second. Here was my chance. If there is one thing women hate, it is a rat. Mother always used to say, "If you want to succeed in life, please the women. They are the real bosses. The men don't count." By eliminating this rodent I should earn the gratitude and esteem of Peter's mother, and, if I did that, it did not matter what Peter's father thought of me.

I sprang.

The rat hadn't a chance to get away. I was right on to him. I got hold of his neck, gave him a couple of shakes, and chucked him across the room. Then I ran across to finish him off.

Just as I reached him, he sat up and barked at me. I was never so taken aback in my life. I pulled up short and stared at him.

"I'm sure I beg your pardon, sir," I said apologetically. "I thought you were a rat."

And then everything broke loose. Somebody got me by the

collar, somebody else hit me on the head with a parasol, and somebody else kicked me in the ribs. Everybody talked and shouted at the same time.

"Poor darling Toto!" cried the visitor, snatching up the little animal. "Did the great savage brute try to murder you!"

"So absolutely unprovoked!"

"He just flew at the poor little thing!"

It was no good my trying to explain. Any dog in my place would have made the same mistake. The creature was a toy-dog of one of those extraordinary breeds—a prize-winner and champion, and so on, of course, and worth his weight in gold. I would have done better to bite the visitor than Toto. That much I gathered from the general run of the conversation, and then, having discovered that the door was shut, I edged under the sofa. I was embarrassed.

"That settles it!" said Peter's mother. "The dog is not safe. He must be shot."

Peter gave a yell at this, but for once he didn't swing the voting an inch.

"Be quiet, Peter," said his mother. "It is not safe for you to have such a dog. He may be mad."

Women are very unreasonable.

Toto, of course, wouldn't say a word to explain how the mistake arose. He was sitting on the visitor's lap, shrieking about what he would have done to me if they hadn't separated us.

Somebody felt cautiously under the sofa. I recognized the shoes of Weeks, the butler. I suppose they had rung for him to come and take me, and I could see that he wasn't half liking it. I was sorry for Weeks who was a friend of mine, so I licked his hand, and that seemed to cheer him up a whole lot.

"I have him now, madam," I heard him say.

"Take him to the stables and tie him up, Weeks, and tell one of the men to bring his gun and shoot him. He is not safe."

A few minutes later I was in an empty stall, tied up to the manger.

It was all over. It had been pleasant while it lasted, but I had reached the end of my tether now. I don't think I was frightened, but a sense of pathos stole over me. I had meant so well. It seemed as if good intentions went for nothing in this world. I had tried so hard to please everybody, and this was the result—tied up in a dark stable, waiting for the end.

The shadows lengthened in the stable-yard, and still nobody came. I began to wonder if they had forgotten me, and presently, in spite of myself, a faint hope began to spring up inside me that this might mean that I was not to be shot after all. Perhaps Toto at the eleventh hour had explained everything.

And then footsteps sounded outside, and the hope died away. I shut my eyes.

Somebody put his arms round my neck, and my nose touched a warm cheek. I opened my eyes. It was not the man with the gun come to shoot me. It was Peter. He was breathing very hard, and he had been crying.

"Quiet!" he whispered.

He began to untie the rope.

"You must keep quite quiet, or they will hear us, and then we shall be stopped. I'm going to take you into the woods, and we'll walk and walk until we come to the city I told you about that's all gold and diamonds, and we'll live there for the rest of our lives, and no one will be able to hurt us. But you must keep very quiet."

He went to the stable-gate and looked out. Then he gave a little whistle to me to come after him. And we started out to find the city.

The woods were a long way away, down a hill of long grass and across a stream; and we went very carefully, keeping in the shadows and running across the open spaces. And every now and then we would stop and look back, but there was nobody to be seen. The sun was setting, and everything was very cool and quiet.

Presently we came to the stream and crossed it by a little wooden bridge, and then we were in the woods, where nobody could see us.

I had never been in the woods before, and everything was very new and exciting to me. There were squirrels and rabbits and birds, more than I had ever seen in my life, and little things that buzzed and flew and tickled my ears. I wanted to rush about and look at everything, but Peter called to me, and I came to heel. He knew where we were going, and I didn't, so I let him lead.

We went very slowly. The wood got thicker and thicker the farther we got into it. There were bushes that were difficult to push through, and long branches, covered with thorns, that reached out at you and tore at you when you tried to get away. And soon it was quite dark, so dark that I could see nothing, not even Peter, though he was so close. We went slower and slower, and the darkness was full of queer noises. From time to time Peter would stop, and I would run to him and put my nose in his hand. At first he patted me, but after awhile he did not pat me any more, but just gave me his hand to lick, as if it was too much for him to lift it. I think he was getting very tired. He was quite a small boy and not strong, and we had walked a long way.

It seemed to be getting darker and darker. I could hear the sound of Peter's footsteps, and they seemed to drag as he forced his way through the bushes. And then, quite suddenly, he sat down without any warning, and when I ran up I heard him crying.

I suppose there are lots of dogs who would have known

exactly the right thing to do, but I could not think of anything except to put my nose against his cheek and whine. He put his arm round my neck, and for a long time we stayed like that, saying nothing. It seemed to comfort him, for after a time he stopped crying.

I did not bother him by asking about the wonderful city where we were going, for he was so tired. But I could not help wondering if we were near it. There was not a sign of any city, nothing but darkness and odd noises and the wind singing in the trees. Curious little animals, such as I had never smelt before, came creeping out of the bushes to look at us. I would have chased them, but Peter's arm was round my neck and I could not leave him. But when something that smelt like a rabbit came so near that I could have reached out a paw and touched it, I turned my head and snapped and then they all scurried back into the bushes and there were no more noises.

There was a long silence. Then Peter gave a great gulp.

"I'm not frightened," he said. "I'm not!"

I shoved my head closer against his chest. There was another silence for a long time.

"I'm going to pretend we have been captured by brigands," said Peter at last. "Are you listening? There were three of them, great big men with beards and they crept up behind me and snatched me up and took me out here to their lair. This is their lair. One was called Dick, the other's names were Ted and Alfred. They took hold of me and brought me all the way through the wood till we got here, and then they went off, meaning to come back soon. And while they were away, you missed me and tracked me through the woods till you found me here. And then the brigands came back, and they didn't know you were here, and you kept quite quiet till Dick was quite near, and then you jumped out and bit him and he ran away. And then you bit Ted and you bit Alfred, and they ran away too. And so we were left all alone, and I was quite safe because you were here to look after me. And then—And then—"

His voice died away, and the arm that was round my neck went limp, and I could hear by his breathing that he was asleep. His head was resting on my back, but I didn't move. I wriggled a little closer to make him as comfortable as I could, and then I went to sleep myself.

I didn't sleep very well. I had funny dreams all the time, thinking these little animals were creeping up close enough out of the bushes for me to get a snap at them without disturbing Peter.

If I woke once, I woke a dozen times, but there was never anything there. The wind sang in the trees and the bushes rustled, and far away in the distance the frogs were calling.

And then I woke once more with the feeling that this time something really was coming through the bushes. I lifted my head as far as I could, and listened. For a little while nothing happened, and then, straight in front of me, I saw lights. And there was a sound of trampling in the undergrowth.

It was no time to think about not waking Peter. This was something definite, something that had to be attended to quick. I was up with a jump, yelling. Peter rolled off my back and woke up, and he sat there listening, while I stood with my front paws on him and shouted at the men. I was bristling all over. I didn't know who they were or what they wanted, but the way I looked at it was that anything could happen in those woods at that time of night, and, if anybody was coming along to start something, he had got to reckon with me.

Somebody called, "Peter! Are you there, Peter?"

There was a crashing in the bushes, the lights came nearer and nearer, and then somebody said "Here he is!" and there was a lot of shouting. I stood where I was, ready to spring if necessary, for I was taking no chances.

"Who are you?" I shouted. "What do you want?" A light flashed in my eyes.

"Why, it's that dog!"

Somebody came into the light, and I saw it was the boss. He was looking very anxious and scared, and he scooped Peter up off the ground and hugged him tight.

Peter was only half awake. He looked up at the boss drowsily, and began to talk about brigands, and Dick and Ted and Alfred, the same as he had said to me. There wasn't a sound till he had finished. Then the boss spoke.

"Kidnappers! I thought as much. And the dog drove them away!"

For the first time in our acquaintance he actually patted me.

"Good old man!" he said.

"He's my dog," said Peter sleepily, "and he isn't to be shot."

"He certainly isn't, my boy," said the boss. "From now on he's the honoured guest. He shall wear a gold collar and order what he wants for dinner. And now let's be getting home. It's time you were in bed."

Mother used to say, "If you're a good dog, you will be happy. If you're not, you won't," but it seems to me that in this world it is all a matter of luck. When I did everything I could to please people, they wanted to shoot me; and when I did nothing except run away, they brought me back and treated me better than the most valuable prize-winner in the kennels. It was puzzling at first, but one day I heard the boss talking to a friend who had come down from the city. The friend looked at me and said, "What an ugly mongrel! Why on earth do you have him about? I thought you were so particular about your dogs?"

And the boss replied, "He may be a mongrel, but he can have anything he wants in this house. Didn't you hear how he saved Peter from being kidnapped?"

And out it all came about the brigands.

"The kid called them brigands," said the boss. "I suppose that's how it would strike a child of that age. But he kept mentioning the name Dick, and that put the police on the scent. It seems there's a kidnapper well-known to the police all over the country as Dick the Snatcher. It was almost certainly that scoundrel and his gang. How they spirited the child away, goodness knows, but they managed it, and the dog tracked them and scared them off. We found him and Peter together in the woods. It was a narrow escape, and we have to thank this animal here for it."

What could I say? It was no more use trying to put them right than it had been when I mistook Toto for a rat. Peter had gone to sleep that night pretending about the brigands to pass the time, and when he awoke he still believed in them. He was that sort of child. There was nothing that I could do about it.

Round the corner, as the boss was speaking, I saw the kennelman coming with a plate in his hand. It smelt fine, and he was headed straight for me.

He put the plate down before me. It was liver, which I love.

"Yes," went on the boss, "if it hadn't been for him, Peter would have been kidnapped and scared half to death, and I should be poorer, I suppose, by whatever the scoundrels had chosen to hold me up for."

I am an honest dog and hate to obtain credit under false presences, but—liver is liver. I let it go at that.

FROM MI TRIP WEST BI ME
BY SCOUTIE BUM-BAILY WHEET-LAM LAPIS-LAZULI
LAP-LANDER LICKERIS COZI-COMFORT SEVER FREEMAN
AS TOLD TO E.H. FREEMAN

Scoutie is travelling by motor camper from Massachusetts to Oregon with his family of ten...

(Beginning ov mi tail.)

Fourth of July.

Winding thro' Chicago! Smoke and noise, piles ov fire-whackers on orl sides—too explosive a day for me! (Being used to music, gentle farm breezes, tinkly brooks, and hermit thrushes, I despise orl rattly sounds.) Well, we came to good old Lak Mishigun. Had lunch on its rocky shore, not smooth like Oshun Beach at Duxbury, mostly humps and gullies, very queer, and rarther unhealthy ov aspect... Saw mi first Piggle-Wiggle store in Chicago, a curious affair. But there was a fine park and thousands ov stately edifices. We went quite near the World's Fair palaces and statues, and a terribly tall thin tower with gold lamps at the bottom. Peeps no end, ov cors, and heaps ov guys and stylish coons, orl smiling because ov the holiday, and shops the biggest yet and oshuns ov cars! A sure-nuff city, It, oh dorg!

Then orf among pleasant oak woods, miles and miles ov it—thro' beautifool Lak Forest, on bi Elgin—heading for St. Paul. Then the roads grew terribly jolty, and Davie tore a large square tear in his fine new trousers, and we got so thirsty we most smothered until we reached nice ice-cram cones and then into

Beautifool clean Wisconsin
Spread like an oshun green...

sweet smelling clover, solid fields ov it, acres and acres orl white, a fluffy sight. Piles ov fat cows, too, very serene and contented-looking. A delishus land!

But one never knows (as Uncle Gissing used to remark), our camp that night was in a Gun-field! (I thort it might go orf, being still the Fourth, but it stayed orl night and made very pleasant lodgings.) It was Head-Quarters shooting for the Black Diamond Gun Club, to be accurate... Rarther martial, but safe; the whole barracks to ourselves, and free (a point pleasing to the Doctor who is Scotch, ov cors)... Pretty late to cook dinner, so orl hands entered a stand-by and took hot dorgs and pops, for once. Long streams ov cars shot bi orl night, but no other shots.

Next day Doctor had to leave us for his trane to Oregon. He was rarther changed from Can steerer into a slick gentleman again, mi saks! So, arfter brfst on the pleasant, sunny greensword, at the Gun-field, we drove to the stashun at Watertown, Wis. (not at orl like the one in Mass.). There, Doctor mounted the Chicago, Milwaukee & St. Paul and Bab took the helm.

Well, on thro' the fine green state we went, seeing piles ov pigs, and clipt sheep, and 3 pink cows. We stoped for long drinks and heaps ov pop-corn at Columbus, and camped for the night in a pretty oak wood at Lak Mason in Briggsville. This camp was corled "Rusty Knoll," a delightful spote if it hadn't been for the ten million musketeers! Bux began reading "Lorna" aloud... Kids like it lots (except Pete).

Next day started with swimmings and hearty scrubbings in the lak. (Bux slid into a gummy mire, while leading me across a slimy old log, and then in trying to pull out one foot, she plopped in the other!) Well, on to the road, again... thro' Tomah (where we saw some baby Indians), and again to a most pretty camp ov tall, quiet woods, checkered with dainty log cabins and hi, spashus cooking pavilions with large stone chimneys; also very neat dining-tables under rustic roofs ("rusty ruffs"). And we saw big sweet pink snap-dragons growing, very wild, but not dangerous.

July 7th, our second Sunday on board.

We took our first long hop. It was along U.S. 10 & 12, from somewhere near Tomah, over to North Hudson, thro' Black River Forls, Eau Claire, etc., a good 180 miles, tra la! Well, arfter excellent brfst under the cute rusty ruff, while a nice cow guarded us from the whizzing rail-road close bi (but we're getting very used ov rail-roads!) ...orf we went, Bab steering as easy as an old salt, which ov cors she is. Warm day, but loverly. Heard the peesful church bells, and passed a church where the peeps were singing earnestly, very pleasant. We had church, too, as we sailed along, with Bible reading and hymns on Violetta. Then Bux gave the opera "Lucia," which the kids liked because it is so tragical.

At Black River (it really is black and blue), we stoped for luncheon; then a very long ride thro' bright wheat-fields, with deep blue mountens orl along the horizon. Orful loverly. Everything went nicely except once when the old mean carbraker stoped again, but Bab soon fixed it with a hair-pin.

Sometimes the lands we went thro' looked like Plymouth Harbour, or Buzzard's Bay, so blue with hare-bells, and sparkling with whitecaps. Then rolling steadily on we basked in the fragrant twilight ov this loverly land, and as darkness gathered in, gently and mildly, we mounted over to the woodlands and finerly found the summer place ov the children's cousins, the Somers. Here was a hearty welcome from many delightful grown-ups and children and a small black-and-white dorg, Tito (whom I can't fight, as he is mi host). So here we are, on a pleasant wooded upland with fine views ov the La Croix River. A real stope, at larst! Yum, yah!

TIME OUT FOR BRETH.

Old Thunder-&-lite broke blasting on us that first night at Hudson, and tho' Bux lifted me up to the hi-rum, I just had to whirl and whirl, and plow (in and out over the sleepers) and I even tried to jump out, I most wore everybody out. So Bux tied me to the roof, till the storm calmed orf again.

Well, it was indeed a scrumshus time for orl. No cooking for Bab, tho' she's always gay as a lark to do it. No steering or jolting or rail-roads, just gay woods and a fine beach to play on, and a plump littel brown pony, Miss Sparkle, for the children, and Tito for me, and distinguished grown-ups for Bab & Bux, instead ov rarther chancy tourists. Mi tail, we did enjoy ourselves a orful heap! There was formal dinner at night (for the elders), and pretty good fun, that, arfter gipsy life…and joli altogethers at luncheon out under the trees at a speshil long, long table under the greensword. The children looked orful nice, orl the time, in their fresh gray uniforms and rosy, tan cheeks. Also, Bab & Bux dressed like ladies, once more (tho' their travel uniforms are most *com-eel-fo*). In the evenings, Bux panted the sunset-river, with its lights and islands, and we'd stroll stately thro' the gardens, and converse hily on the porches. Hank, a very joli, ruddy lad, took the Twins on a fishingtrip—he chuckled some telling about it, as they'd yelled and wobbled so when they spied a fish, that they nearly capsized him.

One day there was a grand camp "orl-over." The rock-climbing rope was stretched between the trees in a huge square and orl 40 blankets aired. Also a hearty worsh, which made such a regular gipsy camp pixure that Bux panted it for the Doctor (for Christmas). Then the Can was swept clean (and hi time for it to be!), and orl re-packed, shipper-shape. Some few corlers, quite curious to see the inner workings, dropped in, making merry remarks. And our larst night we had speshil fun bi celebrating (ahead) Bill's 8th birthday. (Note: this was so that the children might have cake which they're permitted only on family birthdays.) We had a right joli feast under the greensword, Bill received a speshil own jar ov strawberry jam (he grinned orful when he saw it) and ov cors there was heeps ov ice-cram for orl.

GUMBO

On July 11th we took again to the hi road, U.S. 10, heading in dead earnest this time, for the Grand Old West. A joli send-orf we had, ov cors, and the Cage looked extra brite for the bathing-suits were flying from the railings. (We lost May's blue one over-board, but another was procured from a western supply-store.)

Very quickly, now, we were in

Minnisota, Minnisota, on the way to North Dakota,

Where the wheat fields gleam like gold...

an orful sweet old state, piles ov laks, and a fresh green carpet everywhere. We camped at Osakis in a skeetery woods where a man gave Don such a huge fish that it had to be pitched away! Next day we were still rolling along thro' beautifool lands. Soon we reached the Prairie and over we went into North Dakota, "Crossing the big green sea." I liked it orful, riding thro' sweet wavy grain-lands. White fluffy tassels grew close to the hiway, a pretty fringe, miles and miles long. And the edge ov the sky ("hurry-zone") to which we were swiftly sailing, was a sorft purple, and about every half-hour a green hill would appear, then gentle farm with lacy trees for protection. This would be a western "clam," or "go-way-sis," not like the Cape Cod clam at orl, I mean just a circle ov very tall trees where a clump ov bildings is sheltered from the great "Harry-canes." (Note: This word is from *harry canis*, harrying dorgs, meaning terrific blow-outs, don't have them in New England.) We went past piles and piles ov cows, and big gold hay-cocks and tall "grain allegators" rarther dull but dignerfide affairs that resemble huge Hood milk cans as they stand, wide distances apart thro'out the country.

Amusemint.

Beside studying the new scenes on orl sides, the Cage Peeps played games freequintly—roadside cabbage, orthers (omitting me), geography—20 questions, cats-cradle (sily, that) and there were pirate tails and witches tails, but no dorgs' tails exsep mine (rarther scary, but kept the children from fites, for if they teased or banged, there'd be no story). Then we often varied the hours with sorft drinks, peanuts, gum—never candy, ov cors, but nice pop-corn and fruit. And whenever Bab would disappear into a

Bakery, a cheer from the Cage, for soon a big carton ov delightful bags would be lifted up over the rails, and a merry snack for the next 10 miles, orf cookies, doughnuts, or crackers, cheese, tarts, etc.

Well, we went thro' Fargo and camped at "Valley Forls," in a most comical tin camp—everything was tin, even the water. (Oh dory for the good Newton Reservoir, or, better, the spring at Journey's End!) We had electric lights full blarst, but orl the fancy nick-nacks didn't atone for the oily ("orl curly") stuff they corled water.

Anyway, we got out from this queer place at early dawn, in hopes to meet the Doctor's trane this day at Bismark, as arranged bi wires. We did hop it, too, over the dear old Prairie. Saw most loverly blue flax, a glinting violet blue, and piles ov ducks, and several completely scummy laks. One poor lak seemed to be burnt down to gray candlegrease, mi saks! Well, we were delayed, for the first time (and this, ov orl days) bi an old mean flat tire—but Bab and Bux crawled round and pulled and screwed and finerly into Bismark we went full sail, and there was the Doctor peesefully reading Pickwick in the Hotel Mackensie. Arfter repairs, and joli marketing, we made for the camp which we were tickled to find was right on the good old Missouri River! A grand feast ensued, then orl hands happily to bed.

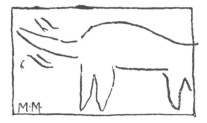

(End ov Mi Tail.)

LETTER FROM NERO TO THOMAS CARLYLE
AS TOLD TO JANE WELSH CARLYLE

Tuesday Jan. 29th, 1850

Dear Master, I take the liberty to write to you myself (my mistress being out of the way of writing to you she says) that you may know Columbine [*the cat*] and I are quite well, and play about as usual. There was no dinner yesterday to speak of; I had for my share only a piece of biscuit that might have been round the world; and if Columbine got anything at all, I didn't see it. I made a grab at one of two 'small beings' on my mistress's plate; she called them heralds of the morn; but my mistress said, 'Don't you wish you may get it?' and boxed my ears. I wasn't taken to walk on account of its being wet. And nobody came, but a man for a 'burial rate'; and my mistress gave him a rowing, because she wasn't going to be buried here at all. Columbine and I don't mind where we are buried.

Tuesday evening.

Dear Master, My mistress brought my chain, and said 'come along with me, while it shined, and I could finish after.' But she kept me so long in the London Library, and other places, that I had to miss the post.

Wednesday.

I left off, last night, dear master, to be washed. This morning I have seen a note from you, which says you will come tomorrow. Columbine and I are extremely happy to hear it; for then there will be some dinner to come and go on. Being to see you so soon, no more at present from your

Obedient little dog, Nero.

NOT TOO BAD
AS TOLD TO JOE WALKER

I'm rather tired. I'm glad it's time
For bed, and, as I slowly climb
Into my basket I must say
I've had a pretty decent day.
Let's see! Two walks, a scrumptious run
All on my own, a bit of fun
With that new cat next door (I wish
Missis would sometimes give me fish),
I missed the dustman (what a shame!)

But teased both postmen, had a game
With several friends who chanced to call,
I bit a hole in my new ball,
I had a doze in Master's chair
(Cook very nearly caught me there,
But I'd kept one eye on the door
And so she found me on the floor!),
I drank the birds' bath almost dry
(The flavour's pleasing—don't know why),
 I chased a rat round William's shed
 But won't repeat what William said
 About his flower-pots (I admit
 That one or two got smashed a bit),
 And... I've forgotten half the rest,
 But anyways I did my best
 To make things hum, and—seems to me
 I've done it quite successfully.
 Here comes my biscuit! That's all right!
 Please kiss me, Missis dear! Good Night!
 I'm dreffle sleepy... would you mind
 Tucking my blanket in behind?

ORIENTAL
AS TOLD TO BURGES JOHNSON

I am Chow—honorable Chow.
Since the reigning of King Kou,
Since my tribe first hunted bear
Up in high Tibetan lair,
Since wild dog first scented man,
Since first dynasty began
Until now,
I am Chow.

I am Chow—Canton Chow.
Mandarins before me bow.
Man's not friend until he's tested,
Dog's not friend until he's bested.
I've been outcast, stoned and driven;
In a palace have I thriven.
Kow tow!
I am Chow.

I am Chow—ancient Chow.
Blue of tongue; furrowed brow.
Upstart white-man I'm appraising;
Shifting feet, I stand here gazing.
Till I choose I'll keep my distance;
No new master's sharp insistence
I'll allow.
I am Chow.

I am Chow—thy dog Chow.
We are bounden, I and thou.
Chang Keng shining down has seen us,
Forged the ancient bond between us.
None within thy house need fear me;
Only if thy cat come near me,
Then WOW!
I am Chow!

NO, YOU DON'T!

AS TOLD TO JOE WALKER

There *may* be a bone on the kitchen floor,
There *may* be a cat at the scullery door,
And it *may* be William has seen a rat,
But, thanks! I shall stay on the hall front mat.
Oh, it's silly the way each one pretends
That he cannot think why I won't budge, my friends,
You're clever, the lot of you, but—I *know*
The car's coming round—and I MEAN TO GO.

CANIS MAJOR
AS TOLD TO ROBERT FROST

The great Overdog,
That heavenly beast
With a star in one eye,
Gives a leap in the east.

He dances upright
All the way to the west
And never once drops
On his forefeet to rest.

I'm a poor underdog,
But tonight I will bark
With the great overdog
That romps through the dark.

FROM HANK THE COWDOG
AS TOLD TO JOHN ERICKSON

BLOODY MURDER

It's me again, Hank the Cowdog. I just got some terrible news. There's been a murder on the ranch.

I know I shouldn't blame myself. I mean, a dog is only a dog. He can't be everywhere at once. When I took this job as Head of Ranch Security, I knew that I was only flesh and blood, four legs, a tail, a couple of ears, a pretty nice kind of nose that the women really go for, two bushels of hair and another half-bushel of Mexican sandburs.

You add that all up and you don't get Superman, just me, good old easy-going Hank who works hard, tries to do his job, and gets very little cooperation from anyone else around here.

I'm not complaining. I knew this wouldn't be an easy job. It took a special kind of dog—strong, fearless, dedicated, and above all, smart. Obviously Drover didn't fit. The job fell on my shoulders. It was my destiny. I couldn't escape the broom of history that swept through... anyway, I took the job.

Head of Ranch Security. Gee, I was proud of that title. Just the sound of it made my tail wag. But now this, a murder, right under my nose. I know I shouldn't blame myself, but I do.

I got the report this morning around dawn. I had been up most of the night patrolling the northern perimeter of ranch headquarters. I had heard some coyotes yapping up there and I went up to check it out. I told Drover where I was going and he came up lame all of a sudden, said he needed to rest his right front leg.

I went alone, didn't find anything. The coyotes stayed out in the pasture. I figured there were two, maybe three of them. They yapped for a couple of hours, making fun of me, calling me ugly names, and daring me to come out and fight.

Well, you know me. I'm no dummy. There's a thin line between heroism and stupidity, and I try to stay on the south side of it. I didn't go out and fight, but I answered them bark for bark, yap for yap, name for name.

The coyote hasn't been built who can out-yap Hank the Cowdog.

A little before dawn, Loper, one of the cowboys on this outfit, stuck his head out the door and bellered, "Shut up that yapping, you idiot!" I guess he thought there was only one coyote out there.

They kept it up and I gave it back to them. Next time Loper came to the door, he was armed. He fired a gun into the air and squalled, something about how a man couldn't sleep around here with all the dad-danged noise. I agreed.

Would you believe it? Them coyotes yipped louder than ever, and I had no choice but to give it back to them.

Loper came back out on the porch and fired another shot. This one came so close to me that I heard the hum. Loper must have lost his bearings or something, so I barked louder than ever to give him my position, and, you know, to let him know that I was out there protecting the ranch.

The next bullet just derned near got me. I mean, I felt the wind of it as it went past. That was enough for me. I shut her down for the night. If Loper couldn't aim any better than that, he was liable to hurt somebody.

I laid low for a while, hiding in the shelter belt, until I was sure the artillery had gone back to bed. Then I went down for a roll in the sewer, cleaned up, washed myself real good, came out feeling refreshed and ready to catch up on my sleep. Trotted down to the gas tanks and found Drover curled up in my favorite spot.

I growled him off my gunny sack. "Beat it, son. Make way for the night patrol."

He didn't want to move so I went to sterner measures, put some fangs on him. That moved him out, and he didn't show no signs of lameness either. I have an idea that where Drover is lamest is between his ears.

I did my usual bedtime ritual of walking in a tight circle around my bed until I found just exactly the spot I wanted, and then I flopped down. Oh, that felt good! I wiggled around and finally came to rest with all four paws sticking up in the air. I closed my eyes and had some wonderful twitching dreams about. …don't recall exactly the subject matter, but most likely they were about Beulah, the neighbor's collie. I dream about her a lot.

What a woman! Makes my old heart pound just to think about her. Beautiful brown and white hair, big eyes, nose that tapers down to a point (not quite as good as mine, but so what?), and nice ears that flap when she runs.

Only trouble is that she's crazy about a spotted bird dog, without a doubt the ugliest, dumbest, worthlessest cur I ever met. What could be uglier than a spotted short-haired dog with a long skinny tail? And what could be dumber or more worthless than a dog that goes around chasing *birds*?

They call him Plato. I don't know why, except maybe because his eyes look like plates half the time, empty plates. He don't know a cow from a sow, but do you think that makes him humble? No sir. He thinks that birdchasing is hot stuff. What really hurts, though, is that Beulah seems to agree.

Don't understand that woman, but I dream about her a lot.

Anyway, where was I? Under the gas tanks, catching up on my sleep. All at once Drover was right there beside me, jumping up and down and giving off that high-pitched squeal of his that kind of bores into your eardrums. You can't ignore him when he does that.

Well, I throwed open one eye, kept the other one shut so that I could get some halfway sleep. "Will you please shut up?"

"Hank, oh Hankie, it's just terrible, you wouldn't believe, hurry and wake up, I seen his tracks down on the creek, get up before he escapes!"

I throwed open the other eye, pushed myself up, and went nose-to-nose with the noisemaker. "Quit hopping around. Quit making all that racket. Hold still and state your business."

"Okay Hank, all right, I'll try." He tried and was none too successful, but he did get the message across. "Oh Hank, there's been a killing, right here on the ranch, and we slept through it!"

"Huh?" I was coming awake by then, and the word *killing* sent a jolt clean out to the end of my tail. "Who's been killed?"

"They hit the chickenhouse, Hank. I don't know how they got in but they did, busted in there and killed one of those big leghorn hens, killed her dead, Hank, and oh, the blood!"

Well, that settled it. I had no choice but to go back on duty. A lot of dogs would have just turned over and gone back to sleep, but I take this stuff pretty serious.

We trotted up to the chickenhouse, and Drover kept jumping up and down and talking. "I found some tracks down by the creek.

I'm sure they belong to the killer, Hank, I'm just sure they do."

"What kind of tracks?"

"Coyote."

"Hmm." We reached the chickenhouse and, sure enough, there was the hen lying on the ground, and she was still dead. I walked around the body, sniffing it good and checking the signs.

I noticed the position of the body and memorized every detail. The hen was lying on her left side, pointing toward the northeast, with one foot out and the other one curled up under her wing. Her mouth was open and it appeared to me that she had lost some tail feathers.

"Uh huh, I'm beginning to see the pattern."

"What, tell me, Hank, who done it?"

"Not yet. Where'd you see them tracks?" There weren't any tracks around the corpse, ground was too hard. Drover took off in a run and I followed him down into the brush along the creek.

He stopped and pointed to some fresh tracks in the mud. "There they are, Hank, just where I found them. Are you proud of me?"

I pushed him aside and studied the sign, looked it over real careful, sniffed it, gave it the full treatment. Then I raised up.

"Okay, I've got it now. It's all clear. Them's coon tracks, son, not coyote. I can tell from the scent. Coons must have attacked while I was out on patrol. They're sneaky, you've got to watch 'em every minute."

Drover squinted at the tracks. "Are you sure those are coon tracks? They sure look like coyote to me."

"You don't go by the *look*, son, you go by the *smell*. This nose of mine don't lie. If it says coon, you better believe there's a coon at the end of them tracks. And I'm fixing to clean house on him. Stay behind me and don't get hurt."

I threaded my way through the creek willows, over the sand, through the water. I never lost the scent. In the heat of a chase, all my senses come alive and point like a blazing arrow toward the enemy.

In a way I felt sorry for the coon, even though he'd committed a crime and become my mortal enemy. With me on his trail, the little guy just didn't have a chance. One of the disadvantages of being as big and deadly as I am is that you sometimes find yourself in sympathy with the other guy.

But part of being Head of Ranch Security is learning to ignore that kind of emotion. I mean, to hold down this job, you have to be cold and hard.

The scent was getting stronger all the time, and it didn't smell exactly like any coon I'd come across before. All at once I saw him. I stopped dead still and Drover, the little dummy, ran right into me and almost had a heart attack. I guess he thought I was a giant coon or something. It's hard to say what he thinks.

The coon was hiding in some bushes about five feet in front of me. I could hear him chewing on something, and that smell was real strong now.

"What's that?" Drover whispered, sniffing the air.

"Coon, what do you think?" I glanced back at him. He was shaking with fear. "You ready for some combat experience?"

"Yes," he squeaked.

"All right, here's the plan. I'll jump him and try to get him behind the neck. You come in the second wave and take what you can. If you run away like you did last time, I'll sweep the corral with you and give you a whupping you won't forget. All right, let's move out."

I crouched down and crept forward, every muscle in my highly conditioned body taut and ready for action. Five feet, four feet, three feet, two. I sprang through the air and hit right in the middle of the biggest porcupine I ever saw.

QUILLS: JUST PART OF THE JOB

It was kind of a short fight. Coming down, I seen them quills aimed up at me and tried to change course. Too late. I don't move so good in mid-air.

I lit right in the middle of him and *bam*, he slapped me across the nose with his tail, sure did hurt too, brought tears to my eyes. I hollered for Drover to launch the second wave but he had disappeared.

Porcupine took another shot at me but I dodged, tore up half an acre of brush, and got the heck out of there. As I limped back up to the house on pin-cushion feet, my thoughts went back to the murder scene and the evidence I had committed to memory.

It was clear now. The porcupine had had nothing at all to do with the murder because porcupines don't eat anything but trees. Drover had found the first set of tracks he had come to and had started hollering about coyotes. I had been duped into believing the runt.

Yes, it was all clear. I had no leads, no clues, no idea who had killed the hen. What I *did* have was a face-full of porcupine quills, as well as several in my paws.

I limped up to the yard gate. As you might expect, Drover was nowhere to be seen. I sat down beside the gate and waited for Loper to come out and remove the quills.

A lot of dogs would have set up a howl and a moan. Not me. I figgered that when a dog got to be Head of Ranch Security, he ought to be able to stand some pain. It just went with the territory.

So I waited and waited and Loper didn't come out. Them quills was beginning to hurt. The end of my nose throbbed, felt like a balloon. Made me awful restless, but I didn't whine or howl.

Pete the barn cat came along just then, had his tail stuck straight up in the air and was rubbing along the fence, coming my way. He had his usual dumb-cat expression and I could hear him purring.

He came closer. I glared at him. "Scram, cat."

He stopped, arched his back, and rubbed up against the fence. "What's that on your face?"

"Nothing you need to know about."

He rubbed and purred, then reached up and sharpened his claws on a post. "You sure look funny with all those things sticking out of your nose."

"You're gonna look funny if you don't run along and mind your own business. I'm not in the mood to take any of your trash right now."

He grinned and kept coming, started rubbing up against my leg. I decided to ignore him, look the other way and pretend he wasn't there. Sometimes that's the best way to handle a cat, let him know that you won't allow him to get you stirred up. You have to be firm with cats. Give 'em the slightest encouragement and they'll try to move in and take over.

Pete rubbed and purred. I ignored him, told myself he wasn't there. Then he brought that tail up and flicked it across the end of my nose. I curled my lip and growled. He looked up at me and did it again.

It tickled my nose, made my eyes water. I had to sneeze. I tried to fight it back but couldn't hold it. I gave a big sneeze and them quills sent fire shooting through my nose, kind of inflamed me, don't you see, and all at once I lost my temper.

I made a snap at him but he was gone, over the fence and into Sally May's yard, which is sort of off limits to us dogs even though Pete can come and go as he pleases, which ain't fair.

With the fence between us, Pete knew he was safe. He throwed a hump into his back and hissed, and what was I supposed to do then? Sing him a lullaby? Talk about the weather? No sir, I barked. I barked hard and loud, just to let that cat know that he couldn't get *me* stirred up.

The door opened and Loper stepped out on the porch. He was wearing jeans and an undershirt, no hat and no boots, and he had a cup of coffee in his hand.

"Hank! Leave the cat alone!"

I stopped and stared at him. *Leave the cat alone!* Pete grinned and walked off, purring and switching the tip of his tail back and forth.

I could have killed him.

I whined and wagged my tail and went over to the gate where Loper could see my nose. He looked up at the sky, took a drink of coffee, swatted a mosquito on his arm, looked up at the clouds again. I whined louder and jumped on the gate so that he couldn't miss seeing that old Hank, his loyal friend and protector of the ranch, had been wounded in the line of duty.

"Don't jump on the gate." He yawned and went back into the house.

Twenty minutes later he came out again, dressed for the day's work. I had waited patiently. My nose was really pounding by this time, but I didn't complain. When he came out the gate, I jumped up to greet him.

Know what he said? "Hank, you stink! Have you been in the sewer again?" And he walked on down to the corral, didn't see the quills in my nose.

At last he saw them. We were down at the corral. He shook his head and muttered, "Hank, when are you going to learn about porcupines? How many times do we have to go through this?

Drover never gets quills in his nose."

Well, Drover was a little chicken and Loper just didn't understand. Nobody understood.

© 1982
G.L. Holmes

He got a pair of fencing pliers out of the saddle shed, threw a leg lock on me, and started pulling. It hurt. Oh it hurt! Felt like he was pulling off my whole nose. But I took it without a whimper—well, maybe I whimpered a little bit—and we got 'er done.

Loper rubbed me behind the ears. "There, now try to stay away from porcupines." He stood up and started to dust off his jeans when he noticed the wet spot.

His eyes came up and they looked kind of wrathful. "Did you do that?"

I was well on my way to tall timber when he threw the pliers at me.

I couldn't help it. I didn't do it on purpose. The quills just got to hurting so bad that I had to let something go. Was it my fault that he had me in a leg lock and got in the way?

Make one little mistake around this ranch and they nail you to the wall.

TEEM——A TREASURE-HUNTER
AS TOLD TO RUDYARD KIPLING

Nothing could prevent my adored Mother from demanding at once the piece of sugar which was her just reward for every Truffle she found. My revered Father, on the other hand, contented himself with the strict practice of his Art. So soon as that Pierre, our Master, stooped to dig at the spot indicated my Father moved on to fresh triumphs.

From my Father I inherit my nose, and, perhaps, a touch of genius. From my Mother a practical philosophy without which even Genius is but a bird of one wing.

In appearance? My Parents come of a race built up from remote times on the Gifted of various strains. The fine flower of it to-day is small—of a rich gold, touched with red; pricked and open ears; a broad and receptive brow; eyes of intense but affable outlook, and a Nose in itself an inspiration and unerring guide. Is it any wonder, then, that my Parents stood apart from the generality? Yet I would not make light of those worthy-artisans who have to be trained by Persons to the pursuit of Truffles. They are of many stocks and possess many virtues, but not the Nose—that gift which is incommunicable.

Myself? I am not large. At birth, indeed, I was known as The Dwarf; but my achievements early won me the title of The Abbe. It was easy. I do not recall that I was ever trained by any Person. I watched, imitated, and, at need, improved upon, the technique of my Parents among the little thin oaks of my country where the best Truffles are found; and that which to the world seemed a chain of miracles was, for me, as easy as to roll in the dust.

My small feet could walk the sun up and down across the stony hill-crests where we worked. My well-set coat turned wet, wind, and cold, and my size enabled me to be carried, on occasion, in my Master's useful outside pocket.

My companions of those days? At first Pluton and Dis—the

solemn, dewlapped, black, mated pair who drew the little wooden cart whence my master dispensed our Truffles at the white Chateau near our village, and to certain shopkeepers in the Street of the Fountain where the women talk. Those Two of Us were peasants in grain. They made clear to me the significance of the flat round white Pieces, and the Thin Papers, which my Master and his Mate buried beneath the stone by their fireplace. Not only Truffles but all other things, Pluton told me, turn into Pieces or Thin Papers at last.

But my friend of friends; my preceptor, my protector, my life-long admiration; was Monsieur le Vicomte Bouvier de Brie—a Marshal of Bulls whom he controlled in the stony pastures near the cottage. There were many sheep also, with whom neither the Vicomte nor I was concerned. Mutton is bad for the Nose, and, as I have reason to know, for the disposition.

He was of race, too—'born' as I was—and so accepted me when, with the rash abandon of puppyhood, I attached myself to his ear. In place of abolishing me, which he could have done with one of his fore-paws, he lowered me gently between both of them, so that I lay blinking up the gaunt cliff of his chest into his unfathomable eyes, and 'Little bad one!' he said. 'But I prophesy thou wilt go far!'

Here, fenced by those paws, I would repair for my slumbers, to avoid my enemies or to plague him with questions. And, when he went to the Railway Station to receive or despatch more Bulls, I would march beneath his belly, hurling infantile insults at the craven doggerie of the Street of the Fountain. After I was expert in my Art he would talk to me of his own, breaking off with some thunder of command to a young Bull who presumed to venture too near the woods where our Truffles grow, or descending upon him like hail across walls which his feet scorned to touch.

His strength, his audacity, overwhelmed me. He, on his side, was frankly bewildered by my attainments. 'But how—*how*, little one, is it done, your business?' I could not convey to him, nor he to me, the mystery of our several Arts. Yet always unweariedly he gave me the fruits of his experience and philosophy.

I recall a day when I had chased a chicken which, for the moment, represented to me a sufficiently gross Bull of Salers. There seemed a possibility of chastisement at the hands of the owner, and I refuged me beneath my friend's neck where he watched in the sun. He listened to my foolish tale, and said, as to himself, 'These Bulls of mine are but beef fitted with noses and tails by which one regulates them. But these black hidden lumps of yours which only such as you can unearth—*that* is a business beyond me!—I should like to add it to my repertoire.'

'And I,' I cried (my second teeth were just pushing), 'I will be a Driver of Bulls!'

'Little one,' he responded with infinite tenderness, 'here is one thing for us both to remember. Outside his Art, an Artist must never dream.'

About my fifteenth month I found myself brother to four who wearied me. At the same time there was a change in my Master's behaviour. Never having had any regard for him, I was the quicker to notice his lack of attention. My Mother, as always, said, 'If it is not something, it is sure to be something-else.' My Father simply, 'At all hazards follow your Art. That can never lead to a false scent.'

There came a Person of abominable odours to our cottage, not once but many times. One day my Master worked me in his presence. I demonstrated, through a long day of changing airs, with faultless precision. After supper, my Master's Mate said to him, 'We are sure of at least two good workers for next season—and with a dwarf one never knows. It is far off, that England the man talks of. Finish the affair, Pierril.'

Some Thin Papers passed from hand to hand. The Person then thrust me into his coat-pocket (Ours is not a breed to be shown to all) and there followed for me alternations of light and dark in stink-carts: a period when my world rose and rolled till I was sick; a silence beside lapping water under stars; transfer to another Person whose scent and speech were unintelligible; another flight by stink-cart; a burst of sunrise between hedges; a scent of sheep; violent outcries and rockings: finally, a dissolution of the universe which projected me through a hedge from which I saw my captor lying beneath the stink-cart where a large black-and-white She bit him with devotion.

A ditch led me to the shelter of a culvert. I composed myself within till the light was suddenly blocked out by the head of that very She, who abused me savagely in *Lingua canina*. [My Father often recommended me never to reply to a strange She.] I was glad when her Master's voice recalled this one to her duties, and I heard the clickety of her flock's feet above my head.

In due time I issued forth to acquaint myself with this world into which I had been launched. It was new in odour and aspect, but with points of likeness to my old one. Clumps of trees fringed close woods and smooth green pastures; and, at the bottom of shallow basin crowned with woodland, stood a white Château even larger than the one to which Pluton and Dis used to pull their cart.

I kept me among the trees, and was congratulating my Nose on its recovery from the outrageous assaults it had suffered during my journeys, when there came to it the unmistakable aroma of Truffles—not, indeed, the strawberry-scented ones of my lost world, but like enough to throw me into my working-pose.

I took wind, and followed up my line. I was not deceived.

There were Truffles of different sorts in their proper places under those thick trees. My Mother's maxim had proved its truth. This was evidently the 'something else' of which she had spoken; and I felt myself again my own equal. As I worked amid the almost familiar odours it seemed to me that all that had overtaken me had not happened, and that at any moment I should meet Pluton and Dis with our cart. But they came not. Though I called they did not come.

A far-off voice interrupted me, with menace. I recognised it for that of the boisterous She of my culvert, and was still.

After cautious circuits I heard the sound of a spade, and in a wooded hollow saw a Person flattening earth round a pile of wood, heaped to make charcoal. It was a business I had seen often.

My Nose assured me that the Person was authentically a peasant and (I recalled the memory later) had not handled One of Us within the time that such a scent would hang on him. My Nose, further, recorded that he was imbued with the aromas proper to his work and was, also, kind, gentle, and equable in temperament. (You Persons wonder that All of Us know your moods before you yourselves realise them? Be well sure that every shade of his or her character, habit, or feeling cries itself aloud in a Person's scent. No more than We All can deceive Each Other can You Persons deceive Us—though We pretend—We pretend—to believe!)

His coat lay on a bank. When he drew from it bread and cheese, I produced myself. But I had been so long at gaze, that my shoulder, bruised in transit through the hedge, made me fall. He was upon me at once and, with strength equal to his gentleness, located my trouble. Evidently—though the knowledge even then displeased me—he knew how We should be handled.

I submitted to his care, ate the food he offered and, reposing in the crook-of his mighty arm; was borne to a small cottage where he bathed my hurt, set water beside me and returned to his charcoal. I slept, lulled by the cadence of his spade and the bouquet of natural scents in the cottage which included all those I was used to, except garlic and, strangely, Truffles.

I was roused by the entry of a She-Person who moved slowly and coughed. There was on her (I speak now as We speak) the Taint of *the* Fear—of that Black Fear which bids Us throw up our noses and lament—She laid out food. The Person of the Spade entered. I fled to his knee. He showed me to the Girl-Person's dull eyes. She caressed my head, but the chill of her hand increased the Fear. He set me on his knees, and they talked in the twilight.

Presently, their talk nosed round hidden flat Pieces and Thin Papers. The tone was so exactly that of my Master and his Mate that I expected they would lift up the hearthstone. But *theirs* was in the chimney, whence the Person drew several white Pieces, which he gave to the Girl. I argued from this they had admitted me to their utmost intimacy and—I confess it—I danced like a puppy. My reward was their mirth—his specially. When the Girl laughed she coughed. But *his* voice warmed and possessed me before I knew-it.

After night was well fallen, they went out and prepared a bed on a cot in the open, sheltered only by a large faggot-stack. The Girl disposed herself to sleep there, which astonished me. (In my lost world out-sleeping is not done, except when Persons wish to avoid Forest Guards.) The Person of the Spade then set a jug of water by the bed and, turning to re-enter the house, delivered a long whistle. It was answered across the woods by the unforgettable voice of the old She of my culvert. I inserted myself at once between, and a little beneath, some of the more robust faggots.

On her silent arrival the She greeted the Girl with extravagant affection and fawned beneath her hand, till the coughings closed in uneasy slumber.

Then, with no more noise than the moths of the night, she quested for me in order, she said, to tear out my throat. 'Ma Tante,' I replied placidly from within my fortress, 'I do not doubt you could save yourself the trouble by swallowing me alive. But, first, tell me what I have done.' 'That there is *My* Bone,' was the reply. —It was enough! (Once in my life I had seen poor honest Pluton stand like a raging-wolf between his Pierril, whom he loved, and a Forest Guard.) *We* use that word seldom and never lightly. Therefore, I answered, 'I assure you she is not mine. She gives me the Black Fear.'

You know how We cannot deceive Each Other? The She accepted my statement; at the same time reviling me for my lack of appreciation—a crookedness of mind not uncommon among elderly Shes.

To distract her, I invited her to tell me her history. It appeared that the Girl had nursed her through some early distemper. Since then, the She had divided her life between her duties among sheep by day and watching, from the First Star till Break of Light, over the Girl, who, she said, also suffered from a slight distemper. This had been her existence, her joy and her devotion long before I was born. Demanding nothing more, she was prepared to back her single demand by slaughter.

Once, in my second month, when I would have run away from a very fierce frog, my friend the Vicomte told me that, at crises, it is best to go forward. On a sudden impulse I emerged from my shelter and sat beside her. There was a pause of life and death during which I had leisure to contemplate all her teeth. Fortunately, the Girl waked to drink. Then She crawled to caress the hand that set down the jug, and waited till the breathing resumed. She came back to me—I had not stirred—with blazing eyes. 'How can you *dare* this?' she said. 'But why not?' I answered. —'If it is not something, it is sure to be something else.' —Her fire and fury passed. 'To whom do you say it!' she assented. 'There is always something else to fear—not for myself but for My Bone yonder.'

Then began a conversation unique, I should imagine, even among Ourselves. My old, unlovely, savage Aunt, as I shall henceforth call her, was eaten alive with fears for the Girl—not so much on account of her distemper, but because of Two She-Persons-Enemies—whom she described to me minutely-by-Eye and Nose—one like-a Ferret, the other like a Goose.

These, she said, meditated some evil to the Girl against which my Aunt and the Girl's Father, the Person of the Spade, were helpless. The Two Enemies carried about with them certain papers, by virtue of which the Girl could be taken away from the cottage and my Aunt's care, precisely as she had seen sheep taken out of her pasture by Persons with papers, and driven none knew whither.

The Enemies would come at intervals to the cottage in daytime (when my Aunt's duty held her with the sheep) and always they left behind them the Taint of misery and anxiety. It was not that she feared the Enemies personally. She feared nothing except a certain Monsieur The-Law who, I understood later, cowed even-her.

Naturally I sympathised. I did not know this *gentilhommier* de Loire, but I knew Fear. Also, the Girl was of the same stock as He who had fed and welcomed me and Whose voice had reassured. My Aunt suddenly demanded if I purposed to take up my residence with them. I would have detailed to her my adventures. She was acutely uninterested in them all except so far as they served her purposes, which she explained. She would allow me to live on condition that I reported to her, nightly beside the faggot-stack, all I had seen or heard or suspected of every action and mood of the Girl during the day; any arrival of the Enemies, as she called them; and whatever I might gather from their gestures and tones. In other words I was to spy for her as Those of Us who accompany the Forest Guards spy for their detestable Masters.

I was not disturbed. (I had had experience of the Forest Guard.) Still there remained my dignity and something which I suddenly felt was even more precious to me. 'Ma Tante,' I said, 'what I do depends not on you but on My Bone in the cottage there.' She understood. 'What is there on *Him*,' she said 'to draw you?' 'Such things are like Truffles,' was my answer. 'They are there or they are not there.' 'I do not know what "Truffles" may be,' she snapped. 'He has nothing useful to me except that He, too, fears for my Girl. At any rate your infatuation for Him makes you more useful as an aid to my plans.' 'We shall see,' said I. 'But—to talk of affairs of importance—do you seriously mean that you have no knowledge of Truffles?' She was convinced that I mocked her. 'Is it,' she demanded, 'some lapdog's trick?' She said this of Truffles— of my Truffles!

The impasse was total. Outside of the Girl in the cot and her sheep (for I can testify that, with them, she was an artist) the square box of my Aunt's head held not one single thought. My patience forsook me, but not my politeness. 'Cheer-up, old one!' I said. 'An honest heart outweighs many disadvantages of ignorance and low birth...'

And She? I thought she would have devoured me in my hair! When she could speak, she made clear that she was 'born' entirely so—of a breed mated and trained since the days of the First Shepherd. In return I explained that I was a specialist in the discovery of delicacies which the genius of my ancestors had revealed to Persons since the First Person first scratched in the first dirt.

She did not believe me—nor do I pretend that I had been entirely accurate in my genealogy—but she addressed me henceforth as 'My Nephew.'

Thus that wonderful night passed, with the moths, the bats, the owls, the sinking moon, and the varied respirations of the Girl. At sunrise a call broke out from beyond the woods. My Aunt vanished to her day's office. I went into the house and found Him lacing one gigantic boot. Its companion lay beside the hearth. —I brought it to Him (I had seen my Father do as much for that Pierrounet my Master).

He was loudly pleased. He patted my head, and when the Girl entered, told her of my exploit. She called me to be caressed, and, though the Black Taint upon her made me cringe, I came. She belonged to Him—as at that moment I realised that I did.

Here began my new life. —By day I accompanied Him to His charcoal—sole guardian of His coat and the bread and cheese on the bank, or, remembering my Aunt's infatuation, fluctuated between the charcoal-mound and the house to spy upon the Girl, then she was not with Him. He was all that I desired—in the sound of His-solid tread; His deep but gentle-voice; the sympathetic texture and scent of His clothes; the safe hold of His hand when He would slide me into His great outer pocket and carry me through the far woods where He dealt secretly with rabbits. Like peasants, who are alone more than most Persons, He talked aloud to himself, and presently to me, asking my opinion of the height of a wire from the ground.

My devotion He accepted and repaid from the first. My Art he could by no means comprehend. For, naturally, I followed my Art as every Artist must, even when it is misunderstood. If not, he comes to preoccupy himself mournfully with his proper fleas.

My new surroundings; the larger size and closer spacing of the oaks; the heavier nature of the soils; the habits of the lazy wet winds—a hundred considerations which the expert takes into account—demanded changes 'and adjustments of my technique... My reward? I found and brought Him Truffles of the best. I nosed them into His hand. I laid them on 'the threshold of the cottage and' they filled it with their fragrance. He and the Girl thought that I amused myself, and would throw—throw!—them for me to retrieve, as though they had been stones and I a puppy! What more could I do? The scent over that ground was lost.

But the rest was happiness, tempered with vivid fears when we were apart lest, if the wind blew beyond moderation, a tree might fall and crush Him; lest when He worked late He might disappear into one of those terrible riverpits so common in the world whence I had come, and be lost without trace. There was no peril I did not imagine for Him till I could hear His feet walking securely on sound earth long before the Girl had even suspected. Thus my heart was light in spite of the nightly conferences with my formidable Aunt, who linked her own dismal apprehensions to every account that I rendered of the Girl's day-life and actions. For some cause or other, the Two Enemies had not appeared since my Aunt had warned me against them, and there was less of Fear in the house. Perhaps, as I once hinted to my Aunt, owing to my presence.

It was an unfortunate remark. I should have remembered her gender. She attacked me, that night, on a new scent, bidding me observe that she herself was decorated with a Collar of Office which established her position before all the world. I was about to compliment her, when she observed, in the low even tone of detachment peculiar to Shes of age, that, unless I were so decorated, not only was I outside the Law (that Person of whom, I might remember, she had often spoken) but could not be formally accepted into any household.

How, then, I demanded, might I come by this protection? In her own case, she said, the Collar was hers by right as a Preceptress of Sheep. To procure a Collar for me would be a matter of Pieces or even of Thin Papers, from chimney. (I recalled poor Pluton's warning that everything changes at last into such things.) If He chose to give of His Pieces for my Collar, my civil status would be impregnable. Otherwise, having no business or occupation, I lived, said my Aunt, like the rabbits—by favour and accident.

'But, ma Tante,' I cried, 'I have the secret of an Art beyond all others.'

'That is not understood in these parts,' she replied. 'You have told me of it many times, but I do not believe. What a pity it is not rabbits! You are small enough to creep down their burrows. But these precious things of yours under the ground which no one but you can find—it is absurd.'

'It is an absurdity, then, which fills Persons' chimney-places with Pieces and Thin Papers. Listen, ma Tante!' I all but howled. 'The world I came from was stuffed with things underground which all Persons desired. This world here is also rich in them, but I—I alone—can bring them to light!'

She repeated acridly, 'Here is not there. It should have been rabbits.'

I turned to go. I was at the end of my forces.

'You talk too much of the world whence you came,' my Aunt sneered. 'Where is that world?'

'I do not know,' I answered miserably and crawled under my faggots. As a matter of routine, when my report had been made to my Aunt, I would take post on the foot of His bed where I should be available in case of bandits. But my Aunt's words had barred that ever-open door.

My suspicions worked like worms in my system. If He chose, He could kick me off on to the floor—beyond sound of His desired voice—into the rabid procession of fears and flights whence He had delivered me. Whither, then, should I go?... There remained only my lost world where Persons knew the value of Truffles and of Those of Us who could find them. I would seek that world!

With this intention, and a bitterness in my belly as though I had mouthed a toad, I came out after dawn and fled to the edge of the woods through which He and I had wandered so often. They were bounded by a tall stone wall, along which I quested for an opening. I found none till I reached a small house beside shut gates. Here an officious One of Us advanced upon me with threats. I was in no case to argue—or even to expostulate. I hastened away and attacked the wall again at another point.

But after a while, I found myself back at the house of the Officious One. I recommenced my circuit, but—there was no end to that Wall. I remembered crying aloud to it in hope it might fall down and pass me through. I remember appealing to the Vicomte to come to my aid. I remember a flight of big black birds, calling the very name of my lost world—'Aa—or'—above my head. But soon they scattered in all directions. Only the Wall continued to continue, and I blindly at its foot. Once a She-Person stretched out her hand towards me. I fled—as I fled from an amazed rabbit who, like myself, existed by favour and accident.

Another Person coming upon me threw stones. This turned me away from the Wall and so broke its attraction. I subsided into an aimless limp of hours, until some woods that seemed familiar received me into their shades...

I found me at the back of the large white Château in the hollow, which I had seen only once, far off, on the first day of my arrival in this world. I looked down through bushes on to ground divided by strips of still water and stone. Here were birds, bigger than turkeys, with enormous voices and tails which they raised one against the other, while a white-haired She-Person dispensed them food from a pan she held between sparkling hands. My Nose told me that she was unquestionably of race—descended from champion strains. I would have crawled nearer, but the greedy birds forbade. I retreated uphill into the woods, and, moved by I know not what agonies of frustration and bewilderment, threw up my head and lamented.

The harsh imperative call of my Aunt cut through my-self-pity. I found her on duty in pastures still bounded by that Wall which encircled my world. She charged me at once with having some disreputable affair, and, for its sake, deserting my post with the Girl. I could but pant. Seeing, at last, my distress, she said, 'Have you been seeking that lost world of yours?' Shame closed my mouth. She continued, in softer tones, 'Except when it concerns My Bone, do not take all that I say at full-fang. There are others as foolish as you. Wait my return.'

She left me with an affectation, almost a coquetry, of extreme fatigue. To her charge had been added a new detachment of sheep who wished to escape. They had scattered into separate crowds, each with a different objective and a different speed. My Aunt, keeping the high ground, allowed them to disperse, till her terrible voice, thrice lifted, brought them to halt.

Then, in one long loop of flight, my Aunt, a dumb fury lying wide on their flank, swept down with a certainty, a speed, and a calculation which almost reminded me of my friend the Vicomte. Those diffuse and errant imbeciles reunited and inclined away from her in a mob of mixed smells and outcries—to find themselves exquisitely penned in an angle of the fence, my Aunt, laid flat at full length, facing them! One after another their heads dropped and they resumed their eternal business of mutton-making.

My Aunt came back, her affectation of decrepitude heightened to heighten her performance. —And who was I, an Artist also, to mock her?

'You wonder why my temper is not of the bluntest?' she said. '*You* could not have done that!'

'But at least I can appreciate it,' I cried. 'It was superb! It was unequalled! It was faultless! You did not even nip one of them.'

'With sheep that is to confess failure,' she said. 'Do *you*, then, gnaw your Truffles?' It was the first time that she had ever admitted their existence! My genuine admiration, none the worse for a little flattery, opened her heart. She spoke of her youthful triumphs at sheep herding expositions; of rescues of lost lambs, or incapable mothers found reversed in ditches. Oh, she was all an Artist, my thin-flanked, haggard-eyed Aunt by enforced adoption. She even let me talk of the Vicomte!

Suddenly (the shadows had stretched) she leaped, with a grace I should never have suspected, on to a stone wall and stood long at far gaze. 'Enough of this nonsense,' she said brutally. 'You are rested now. Get to your work. If you could see, my Nephew, you would observe the Ferret and the Goose walking there, three fields distant. They have come again for My Bone. They will keep to the path made for Persons. Go at once to the cottage before they arrive and-do what you can to harass them. Run—run—mountebank of a yellow imbecile that you are!'

I turned on my tail, as We say, and took the direct line through my well-known woods at my utmost speed since her orders dispatched me without loss of dignity towards my heart's one desire. And I was received by Him, and by the Girl with unfeigned rapture. They passed me from one to the other like the rarest of Truffles; rebuked me, not too severely, for my long absence; felt me for possible injuries from traps; brought me bread and milk, which I sorely needed; and by a hundred delicate attentions showed me the secure place I occupied in their hearts. I gave my dignity to the cats, and it is not too much to say that we were all engaged in a veritable *pas de trois* when a shadow fell across our threshold and the Twc Enemies most rudely entered!

I conceived, and gave vent to instant detestation which, for a while, delayed their attack. When it came, He and the Girl accepted it as yoked oxen receive the lash across the eyes—with the piteous dignity which Earth, having so little to give them, bestows upon her humbles. Like oxen, too, they backed side by side and pressed closer together. I renewed my comminations from every angle as I saw how these distracted my adversaries. They then pointed passionately to me and my pan of bread and milk which joy had prevented me from altogether emptying. Their tongues I felt were foul with reproach.

At last He spoke. He mentioned my name more than once, but always (I could tell) in my defence. The Girl backed His point. I assisted with—and it was something—all that I had ever heard in my lost world from the *sans-kennailerie* of the Street of the Fountain. The Enemies renewed the charge. Evidently my Aunt was right. Their plan was to take the Girl away in exchange for pieces of paper. I saw the Ferret wave a paper beneath His nose. He shook His head and launched that peasant's 'No,' which is one in all languages.

Here I applauded vehemently, continuously, monotonously, on a key which, also, I had learned in the Street of the Fountain. Nothing could have lived against it. The Enemies threatened, I could feel, some prodigious action or another; but at last they marched out of our presence. I escorted them to the charcoal-heap—the limit of our private domain—in a silence charged with possibilities for their thick ankles.

I returned to find my Two sunk in distress, but upon my account. I think they feared I might run away again, for they shut the door. They frequently and tenderly repeated my name, which, with them, was *'Teem.'* Finally He took a Thin Paper from the chimney-piece, slid me into His outside pocket and walked swiftly to the Village, which I had never smelt before.

In a place where a She-Person was caged behind bars, He exchanged the Thin Paper for one which he laid under my nose, saying 'Teem! Look! This is Licence-and-Law all-right!' In yet another place, I was set down before a Person who exhaled a grateful flavour of dried skins. My neck was then encircled by a Collar bearing a bright badge of office. All Persons round me expressed admiration and said 'Lor!' many times. On our return through the Village I stretched my decorated neck out of His pocket, like one of the gaudy birds at the Château, to impress Those of Us who might be abroad that I was now under full protection of Monsieur Le Law (whoever he might be), and thus the equal of my exacting Aunt.

That night, by the Girl's bed, my Aunt was at her most difficult. She cut short my history of my campaign, and cross-examined me coldly as to what had actually passed. Her interpretations were not cheering. She prophesied our Enemies would return, more savage for having been checked. She said that when they mentioned my name (as I have told you) it was to rebuke Him for feeding me, a vagabond, on good bread and milk, when I did not, according to Monsieur Law, belong to Him. (She herself, she added, had often been shocked by His extravagance in this regard.) I pointed out that my Collar now disposed of inconvenient questions. So much she ungraciously conceded, but—I had described the scene to her—argued that He had taken the Thin Paper out of its hiding-place because I had cajoled Him with my 'lapdog's tricks,' and that, in default of that Paper, He would go without food, as well as without what he burned under His nose, which to Him would be equally serious.

I was aghast. 'But, Ma Tante,' I pleaded, 'show me—make me any way to teach Him that the earth on which He walks so loftily can fill His chimneys with Thin Papers, and I promise you that She shall eat chicken!' My evident sincerity—perhaps, too, the finesse of my final appeal—shook her. She mouthed a paw in thought.

'You have shown Him those wonderful underground-things of yours?' she resumed.

'But often. And to your Girl also. They thought they were stones to throw. It is because of my size that I am not taken seriously.' I would have lamented, but she struck me down. Her Girl was coughing.

'Be silent, unlucky that you are! Have you shown your Truffles, as you call them, to anyone else?'

'Those Two are all I have ever met in this world, my Aunt.'

'That was true till yesterday,' she replied. 'But at the back of the Château —this afternoon—eh?' (My friend the Vicomte was right when he warned me that all elderly Shes have six ears and ten noses. And the older the more!)

'I saw that Person only from a distance. You know her, then, my Aunt?'

'If I know Her! She met me once when I was lamed by thorns under my left heel-pad. She stopped me. She took them out. She also put her hand on my head.'

'Alas, I have not your charms!' I riposted.

'Listen, before my temper snaps, my Nephew. She has returned to her Château. Lay one of those things that you say you find, at her feet. I do not credit your tales about them, but it is possible that She may. *She* is of race. She knows all. She may make you that way for which you ask so loudly. It is only a chance. But, if it succeeds, and My Bone does *not* eat the chickens you have promised her, I will, for sure, tear out your throat.'

'My Aunt,' I replied, 'I am infinitely obliged You have, at least, shown me a way. What a pity you were born with so many thorns under your tongue!' And I fled to take post at the foot of His bed, where I slept vigorously—for I had lived that day!—till time to bring Him His morning boots.

We then went to our charcoal. As official Guardian of the Coat I permitted myself no ex-cursions till He was busied stopping the vents of little flames on the flanks of the mound. Then I moved towards a patch of ground which I had noted long ago. On my way, a chance of the air told me that the Born One of the Chateau was walking on the verge of the wood. I fled to my patch, which was even more fruitful than I had thought. I had unearthed several Truffles when the sound of her tread hardened on the bare ground beneath the trees. Selecting my largest and ripest, I bore it reverently towards her, dropped it in her path, and took a pose of humble devotion. Her Nose informed her before her eyes. I saw it wrinkle and sniff deliciously. She stooped and with sparkling hands lifted my gift to smell. Her sympathetic appreciation emboldened me to pull the fringe of her clothes in the direction of my little store exposed beneath the oak. She knelt and, rapturously inhaling their aroma, transferred them to a small basket on her arm. (All Born Ones bear such baskets when they walk upon their own earths.)

Here He called my name. I replied at once that I was coming, but that matters of the utmost importance held me for the moment. We moved on together, the Born One and I, and found Him beside His coat setting apart for me my own bread and cheese. We lived, we two, each always in the other's life!

I had often seen that Pierrounet my Master, who delivered me to strangers, uncover and bend at the side-door of the Château in my lost world over yonder. At no time was he beautiful. But He— My Own Bone to me!—though He too was uncovered, stood beautifully erect and as a peasant of race should bear himself when He and His are not being tortured by Ferrets or Geese. For a short time, He and the Born One did not concern themselves with me. They were obviously of old acquaintance. She spoke; she waved her sparkling hands; she laughed. He responded gravely, at digni- fied ease, like my friend the Vicomte. Then I heard my name many times. I fancy He may have told her something of my appearance in this world. (We peasants do not tell all to *any* one.) To prove to her my character, as He conceived it, He threw a stone. With as much emphasis as my love for Him allowed, I signified that this game of lapdogs was not mine. She commanded us to return to the woods. There He said to me as though it were some question of His magnificent boots, 'Seek, Teem! Find, Teem!' and waved His arms at random. He did not know! Even then, My Bone did not know!

But I—I was equal to the occasion! Without unnecessary gesture; stifling the squeaks of rapture that rose in my throat; cold- ly, almost, as my Father, I made point after point, picked up my lines and worked them (His attendant spade saving me the trou- ble of digging) till the basket was full. At this juncture the Girl— they were seldom far apart—appeared with all the old miseries on her face, and, behind her (I had been too occupied with my Art, or I should have yelled on their scent) walked the Two Enemies!

They had not spied us up there among the trees, for they rated her all the way to the charcoal heap. Our Born One descended upon them softly as a mist through which shine the stars, and greeted them in the voice of a dove out of summer foliage. I held me still. She needed no aid, that one! They grew louder and more loud; she increasingly more suave. They flourished at her one of their detestable papers which she received as though it had been all the Truffles in the world. They talked of Monsieur Le Law. From her renewed smiles I understood that he, too, had the honour of her friendship. They continued to talk of him... Then... she abolished them! How? Speaking with the utmost reverence of both, she reminded me of my friend the Vicomte disentangling an agglomeration of distracted, and therefore dangerous, beefs at the Railway Station. There was the same sage turn of the head, the same almost invisible stiffening of the shoulders, the very same small voice out of the side of the mouth, saying 'I charge myself with this.' And then—and then—those insupportable offspring of a jumped-up *gentilhommier* were transformed into amiable and impressed members of their proper class, giving ground slowly at first, but finally evaporating—yes, evaporating—like bad smells—in the direction of the world whence they had intruded.

During the relief that followed, the Girl wept and wept and wept. Our Born One led her to the cottage and consoled. We showed her our bed beside the faggots and all our other small dispositions, including a bottle out of which the Girl was used to drink. (I tasted once some that had been spilt. It was like unfresh fish—fit only for cats.) She saw, she heard, she considered all. Calm came at her every word. She would have given Him some Pieces, in exchange, I suppose, for her filled basket. He pointed to me to show that it was my work. She repeated most of the words she had employed before—my name among them—because one must explain many times to a peasant who desires *not* to comprehend. At last He took the Pieces.

Then my Born One stooped down to me beside His foot and said, in the language of my lost world, 'Knowest thou, Teem, that this is all *thy* work? Without thee we can do nothing. Knowest thou, my little dear Teem?' If I knew! Had He listened to me at the first the situation would have been regularised half a season before. Now I could fill his chimney-places as my Father had filled that of that disgusting Pierrounet. Logically, of course, I should have begun a fresh demonstration of my Art in proof of my zeal for the interests of my famille. But I did not. Instead, I ran—I rolled—I leaped—I cried aloud—I fawned at their knees! What would you? It was hairless, toothless sentiment, but it had the success of a hurricane! They accepted me as though I had been a Person—and He more unreservedly than any of them. It was my supreme moment!...

I have at last reduced my famille to the Routine which is indispensable to the right minded among Us. For example: At intervals He and I descend to the Château with our basket of Truffles for our Born One. If she is there she caresses me. If elsewhere, her basket pursues her in a stink-cart. So does, also, her Chef, a well-scented Person and, I can testify, an Artist. This, I understand, is our exchange for the right to exploit for ourselves all other Truffles that I may find inside the Great Wall. These we dispense to another stink-cart, filled with delightful comestibles, which waits for us regularly on the stink-cart-road by the House of the Gate where the Officious One pursued me. We are paid into the hand (trust us peasants!) in Pieces or Papers, while I stand guard against bandits.

As a result, the Girl has now a wooden-roofed house of her own—open at one side and capable of being turned round against winds by His strong one hand. Here she arranges the bottles from which she drinks, and here comes—but less and less often—a dry Person of mixed odours, who applies his ear at the end of a stick, to her thin back. Thus, and owing to the chickens which, as I promised my Aunt, she eats, the Taint of her distemper diminishes. My Aunt denies that it ever existed, but her infatuation—have I told you?—has no bounds! She has been given honourable demission from her duties with sheep and has frankly installed herself in the Girl's outside bed-house, which she does not encourage me to enter. I can support that. I too have My Bone...

Only it comes to me, as it does to most of Us who live so swiftly, to dream in my sleep. Then I return to my lost world—to the whistling, dry-leaved, thin oaks that are not these giant ones— to the stony little hillsides and treacherous river-pits that are not these secure pastures—to the sharp scents that are not these scents—to the companionship of poor Pluton and Dis—to the Street of the Fountain up which marches to meet me, as when I was a rude little puppy, my friend, my protector, my earliest adoration, Monsieur le Vicomte Bouvier de Brie.

At this point always, I wake; and not till I feel His foot beneath the bedderie, and hear His comfortable breathing, does my lost world cease to bite...

Oh, wise and well-beloved guardian and playmate of my youth—it is true—it is true, as thou didst warn me—Outside his Art an Artist must never dream!

FROM BEAUTIFUL JOE
AS TOLD TO MARSHALL SAUNDERS

Beautiful Joe is by his own admission "only a cur." Having been res-
cued from a cruel owner, he now resides with Mr. Morris, a clergyman,
and his family…

I always thought that this was the snuggest time of the day—
when the family all sat around the fire—Mrs. Morris sewing, the
boys reading or studying, and Mr. Morris with his head buried in
a newspaper, and Billy and I on the floor at their feet.

This evening I was feeling very drowsy, and had almost
dropped asleep, when Ned gave me a push with his foot. He was
a great tease, and he delighted in getting me to make a simpleton
of myself. I tried to keep my eyes on the fire, but I could not, and
just had to turn and look at him.

He was holding his book up between himself and his mother,
and was opening his mouth as wide as he could and throwing
back his head, pretending to howl.

For the life of me I could not help giving a loud howl. Mrs.
Morris looked up and said, "Bad Joe, keep still."

The boys were all laughing behind their books, for they knew
what Ned was doing. Presently he started off again, and I was just
beginning another howl that might have made Mrs. Morris send
me out of the room, when the door opened, and a young girl
called Bessie Drury came in.

She had a cap on and a shawl thrown over her shoulders, and
she had just run across the street from her father's house. "Oh!
Mrs. Morris," she said, "will you let Laura come over and stay
with me to-night? Mamma has just had a telegram from Bangor,
saying that her aunt is very ill, and she wants to see her, and papa

is going to take her there by to-night's train, and she is afraid I shall be lonely if I don't have Laura."

"Can you not come and spend the night here?" asked Mrs. Morris.

"No, thank you; I think mamma would rather have me stay in our house."

"Very well," said Mrs. Morris," I think Laura would like to go."

"Yes, indeed," said Miss Laura, smiling at her friend. "I will come over in half an hour."

"Thank you so much," said Miss Bessie. And she hurried away.

After she left, Mr. Morris looked up from his paper. "There will be some one in the house besides those two girls?"

"Oh, yes," said Mrs. Morris; "Mrs. Drury has her old nurse, who has been with her for twenty years, and there are two maids besides, and Donald, the coachman, who sleeps over the stable. So they are well protected."

"Very good," said Mr. Morris. And he went back to his paper.

Of course dumb animals do not understand all that they hear spoken; but I think human beings would be astonished if they knew how much we can gather from their looks and voices. I knew that Mr. Morris did not quite like the idea of having his daughter go to the Drurys' when the master and mistress of the house were away, so I made up my mind that I would go with her.

When she came downstairs with her little satchel on her arm, I got up and stood near her. "Dear old Joe," she said, "you must not come."

I pushed myself out the door beside her after she had kissed her mother and father and the boys. "Go back, Joe," she said firmly.

I had to step back then, but I cried and whined, and she looked at me in astonishment. "I shall be back in the morning, Joe," she said gently; "don't squeal in that way." Then she shut the door and went out.

I felt dreadfully. I walked up and down the floor and ran to the window, and howled without having to look at Ned. Mrs. Morris peered over her glasses at me in utter surprise. "Boys," she said, "did you ever see Joe act in that way before?"

"No, mother," they all replied.

Mr. Morris was looking at me very intently. He had always taken more notice of me than any other creature about the house, and I was very fond of him. Now I ran up and put my paws on his knees.

"Mother," he said, turning to his wife, "let the dog go."

"Very well," she said in a puzzled way. "Jack, just run over with him, and tell Mrs. Drury how he is acting, and that I shall be very much obliged if she will let him stay all night with Laura."

Jack sprang up, seized his cap, and raced down the front steps, across the street, through the gate, and up the gravelled walk, where the little stones were all hard and fast in the frost.

The Drurys lived in a large, white house, with trees all around it, and a garden at the back. They were rich people and had a great deal of company. Through the summer I had often seen carriages at the door, and ladies and gentlemen in light clothes walking over the lawn, and sometimes I smelled nice things they were having to eat. They did not keep any dogs, or pets of any kind, so Jim and I never had an excuse to call there.

Jack and I were soon at the front door, and he rang the bell and gave me in charge of the maid who opened it. The girl listened to his message for Mrs. Drury, then she walked upstairs, smiling and looking at me over her shoulder.

There was a trunk in the upper hall, and an elderly woman was putting clothes in it. A lady stood watching her, and when she saw me, she gave a little scream, "Oh! nurse! look at that horrid dog! Where did he come from? Put him out, Susan."

I stood quite still, and the girl who had brought me upstairs gave her Jack's message.

"Certainly, certainly," said the lady, when the maid finished speaking. "If he is one of the Morris dogs, he is sure to be a well-behaved one. Tell the little boy to thank his mamma for letting Laura come over, and say that we shall keep the dog with pleasure. Now, nurse, we must hurry; the cab will be here in five minutes."

I walked softly into a front room, and there I found my dear Miss Laura. Miss Bessie was with her, and they were cramming things into a portmanteau. They both ran out to ask how I got there, and just then a gentleman came hurriedly upstairs, and said the cab had come.

There was a scene of great confusion and hurry, but in a few minutes it was all over. The cab had rolled away, and the house was quiet.

"Nurse, you must be tired, you had better go to bed," said Miss Bessie, turning to the elderly woman, as we all stood in the hall. "Susan, will you bring some supper to the dining-room, for Miss Morris and me? What will you have, Laura?"

"What are you going to have?" asked Miss Laura with a smile.

"Hot chocolate and tea biscuits."

"Then I will have the same."

"Bring some cake too, Susan," said Miss Bessie, "and something for the dog. I dare say he would like some of that turkey left from dinner."

If I had had any ears, I would have pricked them up at this, for I was very fond of fowl, and I never got any from the Morrises, unless it might be a stray bone or two.

What fun we had over our supper! The two girls sat at the big dining-table, and sipped their chocolate, and laughed and talked, and I had the skeleton of a whole turkey on a newspaper that Susan spread on the carpet.

I was very careful not to drag it about, and Miss Bessie laughed at me till the tears came in her eyes. "That dog is a gentleman," she said; "see how he holds the bones on the paper with his paws, and strips the meat off with his teeth. Oh Joe, Joe, you are a funny dog! And you are having a funny supper. I have heard of quail on toast, but I never heard of turkey on newspaper."

"Hadn't we better go to bed?" said Miss Laura, when the hall clock struck eleven.

"Yes, I suppose we had," said Miss Bessie. "Where is this animal to sleep?"

"I don't know," said Miss Laura; "he sleeps in the stable at home, or in the kennel with Jim."

"Suppose Susan makes him a nice bed by the kitchen stove," said Miss Bessie.

Susan made the bed, but I was not willing to sleep in it. I barked so loudly when they shut me up alone, that they had to let me go upstairs with them.

Miss Laura was almost angry with me, but I could not help it. I had come to protect her, and I wasn't going to leave her, if I could help it.

Miss Bessie had a handsomely furnished room, with a soft carpet on the floor, and pretty curtains at the windows. There were two single beds in it, and the girls dragged them close together, so that they could talk after they got in bed.

Before Miss Bessie put the light, she told Miss Laura not to be alarmed if she heard any one walking about in the night, for the nurse was sleeping across the hall from them, and she would probably come in once or twice to see if they were sleeping comfortably.

The two girls talked for a long time, and then they fell asleep. Just before Miss Laura dropped off she forgave me, and put down her hand for me to lick as I lay on a fur rug close by her bed.

I was very tired, and as I had a soft and pleasant bed, I soon fell into a heavy sleep; but I waked up at the slightest noise. Once Miss Laura turned in bed, and another time Miss Bessie laughed in her sleep, and again, there were queer crackling noises in the frosty limbs of the trees outside, that made me start up quickly out of my sleep.

There was a big clock in the hall, and every time it struck I waked up. Once, just after it had struck some hour, I jumped up out of a sound nap. I had been dreaming about my early home. Jenkins was after me with a whip, and my limbs were quivering and trembling as if I had been trying to get away from him. I sprang up and shook myself. Then I took a turn round the room. The two girls were breathing gently; I could scarcely hear them. I walked to the door and looked out into the hall. There was a dim light burning there. The door of the nurse's room stood open. I went quietly to it and looked in. She was breathing heavily and muttering in her sleep.

I went back to my rug and tried to go to sleep, but I could not. Such an uneasy feeling was upon me that I had to keep walking about. I went out into the hall again and stood at the head of the staircase. I thought I would take a walk through the lower hall, and then go to bed again.

The Drurys' carpets were all like velvet, and my paws did not make a rattling on them as they did on the oilcloth in the Morris house. I crept down the stairs like a cat, and walked along the lower hall, smelling under all the doors, listening as I went. There was no night light burning down here, and it was quite dark, but if there had been any strange person about I should have smelled him.

I was surprised when I got near the farther end of the hall, to see a tiny gleam of light shine for an instant from under the dining-room door. Then it went away again. The dining-room was the place to eat. Surely none of the people in the house would be there after the supper we had. I went and sniffed under the door. There was a smell there; a strong smell like beggars and poor people. It smelled like Jenkins. It was Jenkins.

HOW WE CAUGHT THE BURGLAR

What was the wretch doing in the house with my dear Miss Laura? I thought I should go crazy. I scratched at the door, and barked and yelped. I sprang up on it, and though I was quite a heavy dog by this time, I felt as light as a feather.

It seemed to me that I should go mad if I could not get that door open. Every few seconds I stopped and put my head down to the doorsill to listen. There was a rushing about inside the room, and a chair fell over, and some one seemed to be getting out of the window.

This made me worse than ever. I did not stop to think that I was only a medium-sized dog, and that Jenkins would probably kill me, if he got his hands on me. I was so furious that I thought only of getting hold of him.

In the midst of the noise that I made, there was a screaming and a rushing to and fro upstairs. I ran up and down the hall, and half-way up the steps and back again. I did not want Miss Laura to come down, but how was I to make her understand? There she was, in her white gown, leaning over the railing, and holding back her long hair, her face a picture of surprise and alarm.

"The dog has gone mad," screamed Miss Bessie. "Nurse, pour a pitcher of water on him."

The nurse was more sensible. She ran downstairs, her night-cap flying, and a blanket that she had seized from her bed trailing behind her. "There are thieves in the house," she shouted at the top of her voice, "and the dog has found it out."

She did not go near the dining-room door, but threw open the front one, crying, "Policeman! Policeman! help, help, thieves, murder!"

Such a screaming as that old woman made! She was worse than I was. I dashed by her, out through the hall door, and away down to the gate, where I heard some one running. I gave a few loud yelps to call Jim, and leaped the gate as the man before me had done.

There was something savage in me that night. I think it must have been the smell of Jenkins. I felt as if I could tear him to pieces. I have never felt so wicked since. I was hunting him, as he had hunted me and my mother, and the thought gave me pleasure.

Old Jim soon caught up with me, and I gave him a push with my nose, to let him know I was glad he had come. We rushed swiftly on, and at the corner caught up with the miserable man who was running away from us.

I gave an angry growl, and jumping up, bit at his leg. He turned around, and though it was not a very bright night, there was light enough for me to see the ugly face of my old master.

He seemed so angry to think that Jim and I dared to snap at him. He caught up a handful of stones, and with some bad words threw them at us. Just then, away in front of us, was a queer whistle, and then another one like it behind us. Jenkins made a strange noise in his throat, and started to run down a side street, away from the direction of the two whistles.

I was afraid that he was going to get away, and though I could not hold him, I kept springing up on him, and once I tripped him up. Oh, how furious he was! He kicked me against the side of a wall, and gave me two or three hard blows with a stick that he caught up.

I would not give in, though I could scarcely see him for the blood that was running over my eyes. Old Jim got so angry whenever Jenkins touched me, that he ran up behind and nipped his calves, to make him turn on him.

Soon Jenkins came to a high wall, where he stopped, and with a hurried look behind, began to climb over it. The wall was too high for me to jump. He was going to escape. What should I do? I barked as loudly as I could for some one to come, and then sprang up and held him by the leg as he was getting over.

I had such a grip, that I went over the wall with him, and left Jim on the other side. Jenkins fell on his face in the earth. Then he got up, and with a look of deadly hatred on his face pounced upon me. If help had not come, I think he would have dashed out my brains against the wall, as he dashed out my poor little brothers' against the horse's stall. But just then there was a running sound. Two men came down the street and sprang upon the wall, just where Jim was leaping up and down and barking in distress.

I saw at once by their uniform and the clubs in their hands, that they were policemen. In one short instant they had hold of Jenkins. He gave up then, but he stood snarling at me like an ugly dog. "If it hadn't been for that cur, I'd never a been caught. Why—" and he staggered back and uttered a bad word, "it's me own dog."

"More shame to you," said one of the policemen sternly; "what have you been up to at this time of night, to have your own dog and a quiet minister's spaniel dog a-chasing you through the street?"

Jenkins began to swear and would not tell anything. There was a house in the garden, and just at this minute some one opened a window and called out: "Hallo, there, what are you doing?"

"We're catching a thief, sir," said one of the policemen, "leastwise I think that's what he's been up to. Could you throw us down a bit of rope? We've no handcuffs here, and one of us has to go to the lock-up and the other to Washington Street, where there's a woman yelling blue murder; hurry up, please, sir."

The gentleman threw down a rope, and in two minutes Jenkins' wrists were tied together, and he was walked through the gate, saying bad words as fast as he could to the policeman who was leading him. "Good dogs," said the other policeman to Jim and me. Then he ran up the street and we followed him.

As we hurried along Washington Street, and came near our house, we saw lights gleaming through the darkness, and heard people running to and fro. The nurse's shrieking had alarmed the neighbourhood. The Morris boys were all out in the street only half clad and shivering with cold, and the Drurys' coachman, with no hat on, and his hair sticking up all over his head, was running about with a lantern.

The neighbours' houses were all lighted up, and a good many people were hanging out of their windows and opening their doors, and calling to each other to know what all this noise meant.

When the policeman appeared with Jim and me at his heels, quite a crowd gathered around him to hear his part of the story. Jim and I dropped on the ground panting as hard as we could, and with little streams of water running from our tongues. We were both pretty well used up. Jim's back was bleeding in several places from the stones that Jenkins had thrown at him, and I was a mass of bruises.

Presently we were discovered, and then what a fuss was made over us. "Brave dogs! noble dogs!" everybody said, and patted and praised us. We were very proud and happy, and stood up and wagged our tails, at least Jim did, and I wagged what I could. Then they found what a state we were in. Mrs. Morris cried, and catching me up in her arms, ran into the house with me, and Jack followed with old Jim.

We all went into the parlour. There was a good fire there and Miss Laura and Miss Bessie were sitting over it. They sprang up when they saw us, and right there in the parlour washed our wounds, and made us lie down by the fire.

"You saved our silver, brave Joe," said Miss Bessie; "just wait till my papa and mamma come home, and see what they will say. Well, Jack, what is the latest?" as the Morris boys came trooping into the room.

"The policeman has been questioning your nurse, and examining the dining-room, and has gone down to the station to make his report, and do you know what he has found out?" said Jack excitedly.

"No—what?" asked Miss Bessie.

"Why that villain was going to burn your house."

Miss Bessie gave a little shriek. "Why, what do you mean?"

"Well," said Jack, "they think by what they have discovered, that he planned to pack his bag with silver, and carry it off; but just before he did so he meant to pour oil around the room, and set fire to it, so that people would not find out that he had been robbing you."

"Why we might all have been burned to death," said Miss Bessie. "He couldn't burn the dining-room without setting fire to the rest of the house."

"Certainly not," said Jack, "that shows what a villain he is."

"Do they know this for certain, Jack?" asked Miss Laura.

"Well, they suppose so; they found some bottles of oil along with the bag he had for the silver."

"How horrible! You darling old Joe, perhaps you saved our lives," and pretty Miss Bessie kissed my ugly, swollen head. I could do nothing but lick her little hand, but always after that I thought a great deal of her.

It is now some years since all this happened, and I might as well tell the end of it: the next day the Drurys came home, and everything was found out about Jenkins. The night they left Fairport he had been hanging about the station. He knew just who were left in the house, for he had once supplied them with milk, and knew all about their family. He had no customers at this time, for after Mr. Harry rescued me, and that piece came out in the paper about him, he found that no one would take milk from him. His wife died, and some kind people put his children in a home, and he was obliged to sell Toby and the cows. Instead of learning a lesson from all this, and leading a better life, he kept sinking lower.

He was, therefore, ready for any kind of mischief that turned up, and when he saw the Drurys going away in the trian, he thought he would steal a bag of silver from their sideboard, then set fire to the house, and run away and hide the silver. After a time he would take it to some city and sell it.

He was made to confess all this. Then for his wickedness he was sent to prison for ten years, where I hope he will learn to be a better man.

THE DIARY OF SNUBS OUR DOG
AS TOLD TO PAUL R. CARMACK

I.

There's one, very nice thing about my new pillow —

I can move it around wherever I please —

If it's a cold day I put it near a radiator —

Or the big fireplace —

And snooze and snooze!

II.

This afternoon ol' Togo said to me, "How about going to see this little Betty Ann that you have been talking so much about?"

"Suits me", I said - But before we got to her house I warned him about how she likes to sit on one and pull one's tail.

But I guess it wasn't necessary - He's much larger than I am and seemed to enjoy having her use him as a pillow

And when she tried to pull his tail, he just wagged it back and forth and kept it out of her reach

Which is a lot more than I will ever be able to do with the one I have!

III.

Sometimes when ol' Jerry and I go for a hike, he takes me into a field where there's a lot of tall grass and weeds ⌐

And every time I stop to sniff or investigate something ⌐

I lose sight of him ⌐

And instead of being a hike ⌐

It turns out to be more like a game of "hide and go seek"!

PICTURE CREDITS

ACKNOWLEDGEMENTS

"Advice to the Young Dog," from A DOG'S LIFE by Peter Mayle Copyright (c) 1995 by Peter Mayle Reproduced by permission of Alfred A Knopf Inc / "I'm the Dog" by Grenville Kleiser Reprinted with permission from The Christian Science Monitor. Copyright (c) 1940 The Christian Science Publishing Society. All rights reserved. / "Pete's Theology", "Pete's Holiday", from THE LIVES AND TIMES OF ARCHY AND MEHITABEL by Don Marquis. Copyright 1927, 1930, 1933, 1950 by Doubleday, a division of Bantam, Doubleday, Dell Publishing Group, Inc. Used by permission of Doubleday, a division of Bantam Doubleday Dell Publishing Group, Inc. / HIS APOLOGIES by Rudyard Kipling Illustrations by Cecil Aldin. Copyright 1932 by Rudyard Kipling. Used by permission of Doubleday, a division of Bantam Doubleday Dell Publishing Group, Inc. / Excerpt from LUCKY DOG by Ian Hay. Copyright 1934. Used by permission of A.P. Watt Ltd on behalf of Samuel French Ltd. / Excerpt from THE RUBAIYAT OF OMAR KI-YI by Burges Johnson. Copyright 1938. Used by permission of The Putnam Publishing Group. / "Canis Major," from THE POETRY OF ROBERT FROST, edited by Edward Connery Lathem, (c) 1956 by Lesley Frost Ballantine, Copyright 1928, (c) 1969 by Henry Holt and Company, Inc., (c) 1997 by Edward Connery Lathem. Reprinted by permission of Henry Holt and Company, Inc. / "Bloody Murder," from THE ORIGINAL ADVENTURES OF HANK THE COWDOG by John R. Erickson. Copyright 1988 by John Erickson. Used by permission of M-Cross Entertainment. / TEEM-THE TREASURE HUNTER by Rudyard Kipling. Copyright 1935 by Rudyard Kipling. Used by permission of Doubleday, a division of Bantam Doubleday Dell Publishing Group, Inc. / We have been unable to discover the copyright holders of several of the works in this book, and hope to hear from them so that we can make amends and arrange to credit them in future printings.